Ride a Long Shadow

By the same author

The Shadow Rider
Shadow on a Dark Mountain

as Harry Jay Thorn

Hard Ride to Primrose
Incident at Laughing Water Creek
Wyoming Payday Saturday Night
The Sweetwater Kill

*For Edi and Alan
with love & best
wishes Chris x*

Ride a Long Shadow

CHRIS ADAM SMITH

*Chris Adam Smith
Happy Trails
December 99*

A Black Horse Western

ROBERT HALE · LONDON

© Chris Adam Smith 1998
First published in Great Britain 1998

ISBN 0 7090 6290 7

Robert Hale Limited
Clerkenwell House
Clerkenwell Green
London EC1R 0HT

The right of Chris Adam Smith to be identified as
author of this work has been asserted by him
in accordance with the Copyright, Designs and
Patents Act 1988.

*This one is for Jean Margaret Elizabeth
with love and thanks.*

Photoset in North Wales by
Derek Doyle & Associates, Mold, Flintshire
Printed and bound in Great Britain by
WBC Book Manufacturers Limited, Bridgend

Author's Note

Los Almagres, Bowie's Lost Mine. There are those in the Hill Country of South Central Texas who will tell you that the stories you might hear about buried gold, lost mines and fabulous wealth just waiting to be found are all true. Certainly the adventurer, Jim Bowie, was in that part of Texas in 1830 and he spent a great deal of time with the Comanche, learning their secrets and, some claim, stealing their gold and silver. If that is true, it is also certainly true that he didn't take it south to the Alamo with him, which means, as many hopeful treasure seekers believe, it is still up there somewhere. Hidden in a box canyon perhaps or some rocky arroyo just waiting to be found. You will know you are in the right place when you find an old pickaxe driven deep into the bark of a live oak, the handle pointing to the mine's hidden entrance. Bowie did that before he rode off to fight and die for Texas and independence.

Ride a Long Shadow

My thanks to the work of the late William E. Syers, author, historian, newspaper columnist and all-round Texan whose wonderful writings were the inspiration for this story.

Chris Adam Smith 1998

Prologue

Newell County, West Texas 1878

There were four murders across three counties during the late winter and early spring and summer of 1878. The last was in Newell County, close by a run-off creek of the San Saba River. All the murders had one thing in common: they were perpetrated on persons known to have had in their possession information as to the whereabouts of the lost Jim Bowie Mine hidden somewhere deep in the rugged Hill Country of Central Texas.

The first man to die was an old Kiowa Apache, a hermit living in a cave up along the San Sabinas river. The second man to die was a half-breed Mexican known as Charlie Hat to his friends and enemies alike. His real name, however, was Joseph Gomez and that's the name they buried him under when a rain storm washed his decom-

Ride a Long Shadow

posing body from its temporary grave at the edge of a sand spit fingering its way out into the Rio Grande, a few miles to the south of Del Rio. Gomez had sold a supposed treasure map purporting to show the whereabouts of the Bowie Mine. He sold it to Charlie Ackerman, who paid him in silver coin stolen from a bank in El Paso several months previous to his final meeting with Gomez. Ackerman followed the Mexican back to the border and shot him behind the ear with a Remington cap and ball pistol. The ball struck Gomez just below the hairline and popped out through his right eye, killing him instantly. Ackerman, a lazy man, surveyed the hard ground around the murder site and dragged the body to the river where he buried it on an exposed sand bar, digging a makeshift grave in the soft sediment with his hands and rolling the corpse into the hole face down.

From the Rio Grande, Ackerman pushed his painted pony on to the north-east heading, he hoped, for the Hill Country wherein he knew for certain, as only a treasure seeker can, Bowie's Lost Mine, *Los Almagres*, was waiting for him packed with Spanish gold bars and silver ingots stolen from the Comanche, to pick up and pack cross-country to the coast. From there he planned to steamer it on to Califomia and set himself up for the good life. Get him a fine house, a woman –

Ride a Long Shadow

several of them in fact – buy a string of thoroughbred horses, be somebody, dump the rags he wore and the life than went with them. Maybe he would open a bank of his own and stand for mayor. Now that would be something to see.

Such dreams are not new. Since time began, men have searched for treasure and with the seeking of that ever increasing expectation of great wealth, they dreamed of what they would do at rainbow's end. Ackerman rode easily for two days, careful of the road ahead, cautious not to cut another man's trail. He didn't need company, not then anyway; when he got to California, well, that would be a different matter. So he looked ahead and never once behind him to his back trail where Jesus and Paulo Gomez dogged his broken tracks, their thoughts also filled with dreams of buried treasure, but more, their hearts were also full, bursting with hate for the man who had so callously gunned down their brother. That his brother Joseph had stolen the map from him mattered little to Jesus; he was kin and kin was worth dying for – up to a point that is. Only the Gomez brothers had no intention of dying, only of killing. When the moment was right they would bushwhack Ackerman, steal his horse and silver coins and regain the map they themselves had stolen from an old Apache north of where the Sabinas River runs close to Allende, killing the

Ride a Long Shadow

Indian for his food and pony and then, unexpectedly, discovering the map sewn on to the inside of the dead man's baggy, bloodstained shirt.

The Mexicans chose their spot carefully, fearful of risking either of their own lives in the attack. It was early morning, a little after sunrise, when Ackerman rolled from his bedding, broke wind loudly, laughed to himself and, with his hobbled horse in tow, made his way down to the creek, to wash the sleep from his eyes and to fill his coffee-pot with water. He was halfway across a small clearing on the return trip when both Paulo and Jesus opened fire with a brace of five-shot cap and ball percussion pistols. Several of the heavy balls struck Ackerman. Three spread themselves out across his lower torso and one broke his thigh. A fifth shot clipped his left ear from his head, and one wayward ball struck his pony in the head killing it instantly. The animal pitched to the ground mid-stride and lay there, its great flanks shuddering. Ackerman fell heavily, twisted for a moment or two, even tried to rise, to gather his bulk beneath him, before he finally collapsed on to his face, the coffee-pot spilled beside him. The man lay in a pool of dark blood that slowly soaked into the dry sand, but even so, it was several minutes before the killers were sure enough, certain enough that their own safety was in no way jeopardized, that they crept out from the sheltering brush and began ransacking the dead man's trappings, cursing when they did not find the map. And while they searched, Ackerman silently drew together the last reserves of his considerable strength and, as Paulo Gomez leaned over to roll him clear of his pockets, so Ackerman reached up and locked his big hands around the Mexican's throat, pressing the scream from the man with dirty thumbs, the nails biting deeply. Paulo shouted a strangled cry as he rolled across the clearing with the blood-soaked man at his throat. The terrified Jesus yanked the Henry rifle from Ackerman's saddle and, working the lever as quickly as he could, fired off five rounds at the twisting pair. Paulo was killed with the first bullet, but it took three more to stop Ackerman and, even in death, his hands stayed locked around the dead Mexican's throat.

Finding the map in the carbine's saddle boot, Gomez caught up his own pony and put as many miles as he could between himself and his dead brother, the man still lying there in the clearing, unburied and with the murdered gringo's hands reaching out and locked on Paulo's thick neck. Jesus Gomez rode his sad pony hard and to its death. Leaving the dead animal to the coyotes and the buzzards, he shouldered his trappings and continued his journey north. That was when he ran out of luck himself and met up with Rafe

Ride a Long Shadow

Murchison and the Coy brothers, Luke and Matthew, who were heading south and away from a far off hard riding company of Texas Rangers.

Unlike Murchison, who was born and raised in the breaks along the Arkansas River, the Coy brothers were true Texicans from the Big Thicket, raised by a preacher father and a God-fearing mother who, between the two of them, beat the boys into sullen submission and an acceptance of the Bible-thumping way of life they had created for themselves in and around Nacogdoches. When their mother died of the fever and their father took off with a woman who travelled with a quack doctor's medicine show working out of Fort Crogan, the boys headed their slow way west, growing up along the dark trails, hating all that was good in the world and living by the gun and the knife, adept with either in dark alleyways or shadowy arroyos where a man could kill from hiding at little risk to himself. In spite of the hot Texas sun, the Coys were pale of face, rail thin and dressed like scarecrows in raggedy dusters, worn-out boots and with hats that had seen better days on a mule. Their new Colt Army issue pistols were always clean and well oiled though, as were their shotgun and rifle.

It was a bad day for Jesus Gomez when the pair, in the sometime company of Rafe Murchison, a gambler, part-time peace officer and full-time gunfighter, stumbled upon his night camp.

Luke Coy shot the Mexican from the shelter of a small stand of willow trees by a low running creek about twenty yards from the campfire which outlined Gomez against the purple blackness of the late evening, making him the perfect target. Coy used a scatter-gun so there was little chance of the victim being alive when he and Matt broke cover to steal whatever they could find before returning to Murchison and their own campfire several miles to the east and lower down the creek. Yet still they waited for a long while before creeping into the flickering glow of the dying fire. They were surprised to find that their victim did not have a pony, but pleased with the food in his saddle-bags and pack, his Remington pistol, powder and balls and the remainder of the El Paso silver coin. Both Coys were illiterate and could make little sense of the pigskin map wrapped in oil cloth and hidden deep in the man's clothing, tied around his fat belly by a horsehair rope. The case was bloody, but the map was clean. They packed up their spoils and rolled the Mexican on to his own fire, riding out through the dark on their sway-backed ponies as the stench of burning buckskin gave way to the rancid smell of scorched human flesh.

Within the hour, they were back at their own camp fire, drinking weak coffee and poring over the map with renewed attention while Rafe Murchison stood behind them aware of what they had stumbled upon, but unwilling at that point to share the knowledge with them. He had no feelings for the brothers; as far as he was concerned they were merely two extra guns, added protection for the final miles of the long haul down from Arkansas where the climate had become a little warm for him on account of a pretty woman and a gunfight with a local sheriff, resulting in the death of the lawman and the flight of Murchison to pastures new. He had partnered up with them when it was reported that a band of Comanche and Kiowa had crossed the Rio Grande and were hell bent on setting fire to West Texas. Now that they were relatively safe, it was his intention to dump them, but the chance discovery of the map changed that plan, made him reconsider his next move with care. He wanted the map and would kill them if he had to. On the other hand, a brief glance had shown him that their way led through hostile territory and, once again, their guns could back his play against either badge-toter or Kiowa Apache should the need arise.

When asked what the script writing on the pigskin meant, Murchison became a bit vague, telling the pair that it was some kind of treasure map, but that it didn't smell right to him. There were many such maps changing hands at that

Ride a Long Shadow

time as the Apache, Comanche and the Kiowa ran south to Mexico, a lick ahead of the United States Cavalry, or hid out in the hills leaving behind them tales of Apache and Comanche gold caches hidden in the Chisos Mountains, the Chinatis and the wild Hill Country of South Central Texas. Gold, just sitting there waiting to be found. All bullshit as far as he was concerned and he told them that as well.

Murchison had no doubt as to the validity of the map though, even by the flickering glow of the fire he could tell it was genuine, he had a nose for those things – money and fast women were part of his way of life. He reasoned that he could steal the map when the moment was right, maybe lead them on a little at a time, at least until he was good and ready. Riding so far north again was a risk, but the three of them were heavily armed, certainly a match for a Comanche or Kiowa war party – the Apache recently decimated and split into small bands through the endeavours of the army. They could also handle a small company of Texas Rangers should their luck fail them completely.

Murchison didn't think it would come to that, so far his luck had been good and he was sure it would hold. He was a superstitious man and he had crossed a Mexican witch lady's palm with silver in Del Rio, bought her a red flower for her

Ride a Long Shadow

hair. The only bad things he could see about the deal was the delay in crossing the Rio Grande and reaching the comparative safety of Mexico, and having to ride back to the Hill Country. It would take time to organize the search and to pick up the equipment they might need in order to wrest the gold from Bowie's Mine. But he figured he could live with that. He would need more than the Coys' help though. If there were Kiowa and Comanche in the hills, and if there were any truth in the wild rumour that Santana had broken out of Huntsville and was heading west, it would take more than the three of them to see the deal through. Pick up a couple more men maybe; there were plenty of such border trash around, cutthroats and gunslingers who would sell their souls for a smell of Bowie's gold.

That night, when Murchison was sure the two men were happily asleep, he allowed the night and the dreams of gold to take him, wrap themselves around him and comfort his own restless sleep.

The tall man cut their trail the next afternoon. He examined their campsite and then backtracked them to the partially burned and still smouldering body of Jesus Gomez, and then on back where Paulo Gomez and Charlie Ackerman's flyblown bodies were huddled together in a small clearing

Ride a Long Shadow

locked in eternal combat by rigid, blood-blackened hands. He covered his nose against the stink and read the sign, carefully making notes as to the positions of the bodies. Seemingly satisfied with his findings, he cut east for the Neuces River and the Shadow Rider.

ONE

Theresa was raking through the dry earth out back of the house. She was stooped over, her sleeves rolled up on her brown arms, her hair hung loose and down and I watched the gentle movement of her breasts against the low-cut neck of the sun-faded floral dress she always wore when gardening. I loved that woman and she knew it. She must have sensed me staring at her from the back porch seat and looked up smiling and then down to where I was looking. She laughed out loud then, her laughter cheerfully filling the late morning air. A musical sound that in some way, just for a few moments, lightened the burden that had settled heavily upon my shoulders, scratching at me there, pecking away like an old black crow.

'Whatever it is you're thinking, fella, best forget it.'

Then she laughed some more as Jonah came

Ride a Long Shadow

around the corner of the house, a tow-haired twelve year old with more good common sense than most people twice his years.

'What was he thinking, Ma?' the boy asked, with an ear-to-ear grin on his face which I very quickly removed by telling him to help his mother in the vegetable patch, when all he really wanted to do was to ride out with me to White Hat Creek. It wasn't a punishment that I would not allow him to go with me, usually I enjoyed his company out on the range listening to his endless chatter, answering his questions, but not just at that moment. I wanted to be alone to try to think things out, sort out the good from the bad and find a trail for us all that would not end in disaster. He nodded to me, the smile still there knowing, I supposed in his own way, that I needed some time to myself. The problems surrounding our move to the Neuces were shared as a family and even Moke Calloway, the old Negro who had trailed north to Wyoming with my father at the end of the war and was usually to be found at my elbow, kept out of my way on a bad day.

I waved to them, told them I would be home for supper and then, walking to the barn I saddled the bay, fetched my fancy handgun and holster from the house and hung them over the pommel. My left leg was stiff and sore; it always is in times of trouble, something to do with tension is what

Ride a Long Shadow

Theresa's father, Doc Meyer, had told me back in Sawmill. The dapper little doctor hoped to join us in the spring, but we had to wire him that it was not a good idea, the ranch house being in such a run-down state, that and the fact that we had lost most of the herd on the trail up from Fort Worth. Maybe the following year; I hoped so. I ignored the ache in my leg and pushed the bay out across the yellow grassland. We needed rain and lots of it, but the sky was an azure blue, cloudless right away across to the west where the distant ranges were shrouded in a heat-haze, their higher reaches suspended in the hot dry air.

By the time we reached the creek both the bay and me were bathed in sweat and covered in dust. Several steers moved disconsolately about the dry grass looking at me as I rode by, bawling, gaunt, asking for feed and water and I could offer them neither.

I dismounted and ground-hitched the reins, walking the last five yards to the creek. I pushed my hat to the back of my head and got down on one knee and stared across to where the hanging branches of a willow tree dipped their shimmering leaves into the crystal clear water – only there was no water; White Hat was dry as the inside of a dead man's mouth, the mud of its course dimpled with bird prints and those of larger animals, including our fifty head of cattle, the

Ride a Long Shadow

only ones to survive the long haul down to the Neuces River country from the north of Fort Worth the previous summer. What with bad weather, floods and Kiowa, we had been lucky to keep so many. Saving the cattle and protecting Theresa, Jonah and old Moke had pretty near drained me by the time we reached the Bar S which we renamed the Diamond H after my late father's place in Wyoming.

I had bought the spread unseen many years before when I was marshalling under Jack Brubaker in Denver. A kind of romantic notion, a place to go when the sound of gunfire finally stilled and I could head south with my wife, stepson and old Moke to a new life, out from behind the badge once and for all.

But, like most things in my life, it had not run to plan. When we crested the brow of a low hill and looked down on our narrow valley our hearts were full. Below us in the far distance we could see beyond the waving prairie grass to where a line of willows and small cottonwoods ran along the bank of White Hat Creek and, much nearer, just beyond the morning shadow of the hill upon which we stood, we could see the ranch house although it was mostly obscured by live oak and mature cottonwoods. The pole corral was broken and run down, but that was to be expected, the place had been deserted for several years. But it was much more than that. As we drew nearer, Jonah bouncing up and down with excitement on the wagon seat sitting next to Theresa who was a skilled teamster, and with Moke riding Jonah's colt, the full devastation of the place became apparent. One of the barns was burned to the ground and small fires had been lit in the main building; part of the side and front wall were missing or charred and hanging loose. The stone chimney stood tall and intact, but part of a stone wall facing to its left hand side had fallen in. Rooms that were whole had been inhabited by saddle tramps, Indians and wild things and their dirt was apparent everywhere. The windmill was rusted solid and the water tank empty. I could see Theresa fighting back the tears and I have to admit to fending off a few of my own. Only old Moke and the boy were undaunted, telling us both that better things would come out of the ruins and we could redesign it to our own liking. An old man and a boy filled with enthusiasm for a project for which I honestly cared little. What with losing so many cattle, the fact that it would be a long time before we were finally settled in our own home did not delight me.

We had reached the Neuces in the early fall and the weather was beginning to harden, too much I felt for Theresa and Moke, although Jonah and I could and did toil through the most of it. The boy and I with some local help worked through the bad weather, the worst of the winter and, by late April, the spread was looking good with a cedar pole arch at the entrance bearing our brand and the new windmill filling the tank. We bought three new horses, stocked the larder with salt, flour and other essentials and bought new furniture – most purchased from a neighbouring rancher who was heading back to his native Arkansas and who offered us a better than good deal. We also purchased the man's milk cow, a town dog for Jonah and a new dress for Theresa. Fresh stock would have to wait though, as the lumber, the mill and the hired labour had just about run our poke dry. But I took out a loan, enough for two hundred head, from the bank in Uvaldi putting the Diamond H up as collateral. Things were tight but set to improve, and then the summer sun had broken through the spring clouds and stayed there, burning down on the countryside, yellowing the grass and driving the stock to higher ground where, even there, they found little to sustain them. If that were not enough, a dry storm lightning bolt struck the windmill, melting the metal solid and firing the timber. I felt that God had it in for me real bad.

I knew that my chances of making the payment were slim to improbable. The cattle were in no shape to be resold and many of the new-born

Ride a Long Shadow

calves had died through lack of milk from their dehydrated mothers. There had to be another way though, there always is, but I couldn't think of it and making the payment was damned near impossible.

I flipped a pebble over the dried-out creek bed where it bounced on the cracked mud making a hollow sound. There were a few birds scrounging around in a little muddy pool that smelled of dead fish, but that was all. My neighbour, who had three windmills pumping water to tanks on the higher plain, told me it was the first time in living memory that the creek had run dry and that I should sink more wells as he had done. But windmills and wells, together with the drilling of them, cost money which I did not have. I was still thinking about my problems, feeling a little sorry for myself when I saw the rider coming on.

First his tall, flat-brimmed hat broke through the haze, followed by slim dust-covered shoulders. Then the horse, a sorrel, and soon horse and rider were dancing on the heat making for the creek, hoping, I guessed, for water. I watched him carefully as they broke through the shimmer and took on solid form in the shade of the cottonwoods, thinking to myself that maybe I should take my Colt from where it was still hanging on my saddle horn. Then I recognized the rider and relaxed a little. He paused at the edge of the creek, saw me

Ride a Long Shadow

and pushed the big horse along the gravel that ran the sides of White Hat offering, in better years, shelter for spawning trout.

He was a tall man on a tall horse. Six feet two and a good three inches taller than me. He reined the big animal in, shifted his backside on the saddle and leaned forward on to the pommel. It was clear to see that both horse and rider had travelled far and fast.

'You are looking good for an old man, Wes, how've you been?'

I straightened placing my weight on my good leg.

'Tolerable I guess, but it's been a lot of years, Posy, and you are still one damned liar.'

The tall man grinned and slid from his saddle, lifting the stirrup fender and loosening the cinch a little before walking over and shaking my hand. Possum James Tobin was a thin man from the top of his head to his tiny feet. His face was long and pointed stretching down from wide temples to a narrow chin, broken in the middle by a thin nose which sported the signs of at least two breaks. He had sharp, black eyes, a mouth that seemed to span the width of his face, the thin upper lip partially covered by a drooping moustache and, beyond that, four days' growth of grey whiskers.

'You're right, Wes, I am a damned liar and you

look just about as done in as I feel. This White Hat Creek?' He had a deep, nut-brown voice thickened by tobacco and laced with casual humour.

'It was last spring, now it's a mud pool, dried up and blown away.'

'Good, for a while there I thought I was lost. Any other water near here?'

'My place is about two miles from the north of here, I got one tank and a hand pump that's sucking air.'

'It's one hell of a hot summer, Wes, and those steers look about done for if they don't get some good feed and water in them soon.'

I looked over to where a dozen or so beeves were staring round-eyed at us from the shelter of a cottonwood, their hooves making no impression on the baked creek bed.

I nodded agreement.

'You down on hard times here, Wes, or are you just one hell of a bad rancher?'

I hunkered down again and he joined me, shrugging out of the duster and dragging the makings out from the pocket of his faded red shirt. He rolled a thin smoke, fired it with a blue top and passed the sack to me. I rarely smoked, but it seemed the right thing to do squatting there in the shade with an old *compadre* from way back when. The Durham tasted sweet and tickled my throat, but it was a fine moment.

Ride a Long Shadow

'You still with the Rangers?' I asked after a while.

'I quit last fall, it's not the same as it was.'

'What brings you to this part of the country, you looking for work?'

'No, actually I rode by here to see you. I wired Jack Brubaker in Denver and he told me you'd moved down to the Neuces. You weren't too hard to find and Jack sends his regards to you and your family.'

I thought about Brubaker. We had ridden together in the US Marshals Service. He had arrested me one time when a complaint had been made against me and I was accused of murdering a couple of bank robbers who put up more than a bit of a fight when I tried to bring them in. A crooked county sheriff didn't help my case any and I served two years of a life sentence in the Colorado State Prison at Canon City. Brubaker then worked ceaselessly to get my name cleared and a pardon granted. He was successful in both cases. He was the best man at my wedding and took care of Jonah in his cabin up by Cherry Creek while Theresa and I had a late honeymoon. Jack Brubaker was all right, the straightest man I had ever met and I missed him.

'Why would you be wanting to see me, Posy?'

I was genuinely surprised and it was in the

Ride a Long Shadow

tone of my voice. We had ridden together and one time we had shot our way out of a Kiowa ambush with the tall man playing possum until he could get the drop on our attackers. From then on he was called 'Possum', a sobriquet I stuck him with which was usually shortened to Posy. We were both with the Rangers back then before the formation of the State Police, and Tobin was back with them again when they were re-established in 1874 on the orders of the then governor, Richard Coke. I had long moved on by that time though, rode north and joined the Marshals riding under a Colorado warrant and then later, in Wyoming, after my pardon and my father's ranch was burned to the ground. There was some killing up there and I was glad to be away from under the badge, any badge.

'I've got a proposition for you, Wes, one to consider even if you turn it down, but I have to say it looks as though you could use a whole load of *dinero*, my old friend, and that, I can put your way. You interested?'

I straightened and walked to the edge of the creek. I could hear cattle bawling, moving through the willows, and I wondered how much longer they could last without feed and water.

'I'll hear you out, Posy,' I said over my shoulder, conscious of the fact that he was staring at my back, waiting.

Ride a Long Shadow

*

He laid it on me down there by the dry White Hat Creek, his words sometimes confused and mixed in with the bawling of the cattle. He was an intelligent man, a man who had survived countless difficulties. He was a hard man in a land filled with hard men, but he was head and shoulders above them in more ways than one. I liked him, always had, but his story threw me and his proposition, on the face of it, was at first unacceptable. That was only at the start of it though; by the time he had finished talking I was signed up. It was as I had thought when I first arrived at the creek that afternoon, there had to be another course of action and Posy offered it to me. The way he told it was like this.

Posy Tobin had first got himself involved in the search for Jim Bowie's Lost Mine in '76 when he heard the legend retold by an Apache shaman he had rescued from drunken settlers out to beat him to death on account of a stolen milk cow. It was an old enough story even then, but it was the first time he had heard it told with any real conviction. The ancient Apache, his eyes burning in the firelight, told about the lost mine and how Bowie had lived with the Comanche for a year, learning their secrets and then relieving them of as much gold and silver as a dozen pack horses could carry. He sang of the dead, of his old enemy the Comanche who fought with Bowie, and then of the dead Kiowa and Apache who, in their turn, had tried to wrest the gold from the knife-fighter before he hid it, buried deep in an abandoned mine shaft left over from the diggings of Don Bernardo de Miranda, Spanish Lieutenant Governor of Texas way back in 1756. The entrance to the mine was sealed over the bodies of two Comanche warriors who, in one last bloody skirmish, tried to regain their fortune. Before leaving, Bowie stuck a pickaxe into the trunk of an oak tree, the shaft pointing to the mine's hidden entrance, and then he went off to die on the end of a Mexican bayonet at the Alamo mission in company with Crockett and Travis.

Posy had listened quietly, never asking questions for fear the old man would end his story, but the Apache was dying from a wound the Ranger had not seen and, in fact, did not discover until he buried the man the following morning.

According to the shaman, when Santa Anna's men pillaged the mission, a trooper took the map from Bowie's bloody body and handed it over to a wounded officer, Don Renaldo of Chihuahua who, guessing at the significance of the find, took it with him when he was mustered out of the army, a cripple in body but not in mind. The map, drawn

Ride a Long Shadow

on pigskin and protected in oil cloth, changed hands many times in the Renaldo family and more than one expedition was mounted to retrieve the cache. Each in turn was thwarted, sometimes by a lack of knowledge of the terrain or marauding Indians, and at other times by the US Cavalry or the Texas Rangers.

Through the long dark years, the Comanche themselves had not forgotten the duplicity of Jim Bowie and neither had they ceased in their own efforts to find the map they believed was made by him when he first headed south after finally quitting the San Saba for greener pastures. The Comanche never found it, that chore fell to an Apache in the spring of '75.

Renaldo's grandson made one last concerted effort to find the treasure, but the train of heavily armed men was wiped out by a mere handful of Chiricahua Apache who lured the Mexicans into a box canyon and there slaughtered them to a man. The map was retrieved by chance and a warrior named Ten Ponies, a veteran of many battles, was appointed its guardian.

The old man died in Tobin's arms, singing of the dead and the life to come. Tobin had no doubts about the story whatsoever and within two weeks he had resigned from the Frontier Battalion of Rangers, solemnly shaken hands with his chief, Major John B. Jones, and was headed south-west towards the Chisos. After a year of searching, he found Ten Ponies, or rather he found the Apache's body, murdered in a draw, bushwhacked and several months dead. Identification had been difficult, but Posy was an expert on border Indians and he backtracked the man to his hogan hidden deep in the arroyos leading off from the Sabinas River. Satisfied he had the right man, he took up the cold trail of the killers only pausing his search for two weeks in order to raise the financial backing he needed from the Renaldo family.

It took him six months to locate the three Gomez brothers and, when he did find them, they were all dead. Joseph, murdered by a man called Charlie Ackerman who, in his turn, was ambushed by Jesus and Paulo, taking Paulo down with him in what looked to have been a bloody struggle. The remaining Gomez brother ran blind and straight into Rafe Murchison and the Coy brothers, late of Nacogdoches, all three known by reputation to both myself and Tobin as dangerous hardcases.

Posy Jim Tobin did not have the map showing the whereabouts of Bowie's Lost Mine but he knew who did have it. Better yet, he had $3,000 in American and $1,000 of that was mine in advance if I chose to ride with him. That, and the promise of more, much more to follow, decided me and we

Ride a Long Shadow

shook hands on it in the gathering purple dusk down by the dry White Hat Creek, the dying red sun's reflection gleaming darkly in Posy Tobin's black eyes giving his narrow, pointed face a satanic appearance. Somewhere off in the distance across my neighbour's property, a dog coyote howled at the rising moon and the echoing cry sounded like laughter and I wondered uncomfortably, for one brief moment, if he was laughing at me.

TWO

Theresa glowered moodily at me over the supper table. Jonah had worn himself out listening to the tall tales, some involving me, that Jim Tobin told him while they were sitting on the porch waiting for supper, giving me some time in which to talk to my wife and old Moke Calloway. The black man listened in absolute silence, only his moist brown eyes betraying the fear and emotion he felt at my leaving them. Not fear for himself, but fear for my well-being. I tried to reassure him as well as persuade Theresa that what I was doing was the right thing to do. I don't believe I sounded completely convincing, but that was more to do with my uncertainty about what actually lay ahead for Posy and me rather than my decision to go. I could tell from Theresa's demeanour that it sat badly with her that I had taken that decision without first consulting her.

Tobin could eat more food than any man I had

ever known and still there wasn't an ounce of fat on his thin frame. He wiped the gravy from his plate with a slice of freshly baked bread, dabbed his lips with a napkin and excused himself, saying he wanted to rub down his horse and check his tack before the morning. He was riding out at first light and I planned to meet him at an old fort we both knew to the north of Enchanted Rock Canyon. I had a few things to take care of in town before I could ride for the map and the gold.

Jonah took himself red-eyed and tired off to his bed and Moke settled himself on the front porch with his pipe. Theresa rattled the dishes more than was necessary and did not look at me when I walked over to the sink and began to dry the pots and pans. It was not an unusual thing for me to do and the help usually earned me a bright smile and a soft kiss, not that time though. Her back was rigid and her movements mechanical as if she were a thousand miles away from me and never coming back. I put down the drying up cloth and reached for her shoulders; they were like rock. I turned her towards me and I could see that she was close to tears, her wet hands dropping to her sides and then round my waist as I guided her to the table, sat her down and fetched the bottle of good sipping whiskey from out of the dining-room cupboard together with two shining crystal glasses. I sat opposite her with the bottle between

Ride a Long Shadow

us. She was staring at her hands but looked up with the promise of a smile, a break in the storm, as I poured two shots each of the richly amber spirit.

I am not a young man and time is important to me. Unlike Jonah, who sees his whole life ahead of him as one long adventure beyond a distant horizon never to be reached, I cannot help at times but think that I have crested my horizon, reached the top of that great hill of life and, on looking back, see only a faint light where once there had been bright sunshine, and then, ahead of me, a misty path leading to I know not where. They are the dark times and they have ridden beside me more frequently since we reached West Texas than they ever did in Wyoming and Colorado, and yet only two years had passed since we quit the north country ranges for the Neuces. That dark time was with me out at White Hat Creek when Posy Tobin had ridden out of the heat-haze, his eyes afire with thoughts of gold and good fortune. It was with me while I sat there hunkered over the cracked mud listening to the cattle bawling for feed and water and it was with me when I signed the bank loan papers in Uvaldi.

I had given my life to the law in one way or another, saved a president's life, fought in a war of which I really wanted no part, and killed more than my share of men over the open sights of a

Ride a Long Shadow

Colt or a Winchester. I had ridden with the US Marshals Service, worn a sheriff's badge, a Texas Ranger's star struck from a Mexican five peso coin and those symbols of office had offered little in the way of protection or remuneration. From behind those stars and shields, I had been wounded seven times and limp like an old man when the weather is cold or my spirits are running low. I have seen good men fall at my side, visited the graves of others and paid my respects to widows I had never met, only heard tell of them from the mouths of lonely husbands riding in pursuit of men not worth the dying for. Those dark times would be with me more frequently now I knew for sure, but looking across the table at my Theresa I was determined that, when night finally came to me, both she and Jonah would be taken care of. It had seemed an impossible dream until Posy Jim Tobin had opened a door, shown me a trail, and all I had to do was saddle the bay and ride it all the way to hell and back should it prove to be necessary.

I reached out and took Theresa's slim hand in mine. She seemed to read the desperation in me, her dark, troubled eyes staring at me, wanting to understand, to be with me, but finding something between us which I had placed there. I did not know how to tell her of my thoughts but she knew them anyway.

Ride a Long Shadow

'You don't have to ride for Jonah and me, Wesley, the summer will pass and we will make it out here. It's a pleasant land and usually there is good grass and plenty of water. It's only a matter of time.' Her voice was soft and moist tears not too far away.

'Time is something we don't have, Theresa. There are cattle dying out there and we have no money to help them and no means of replacing them when the good times do come back. It's all gone. Riding with Jim Tobin will give us a fresh start.'

Theresa was listening to me but not hearing me.

'My father could help us, he would be happy to. You know that he is fond of you, he would understand.'

There was a desperation in her voice I did not like to hear. It made me feel guilty, angered me. My voice lifted a little.

'I didn't marry you and take on Jonah to go running back to your father the moment things got tough for us. We can make it on our own and I will see to it that you never want again.'

And there it was out in the open – the gold. Theresa, I knew, saw a fire, a hunger in me at that moment that had little to do with pride, the ranch or the flickering glow of the oil lamp, and I looked away, let go of her hand and walked to the dead

Ride a Long Shadow

fireplace. The big dressed key-stone had come from my father's burned-out ranch house and I wondered, as I often did in times of trouble, what he would say, how he would advise me on whether or not my proposed course of action was the correct one. He was a wise, far thinking old man and I kidded myself he would tell me to go with the gold and even though I really knew better, I denied that knowledge.

'Is that what it's really about, Wes, Indian gold?'

I turned back to my wife and our eyes met across a distance I could not cover.

'That's part of it, I suppose, but not all of it. Sure, I wouldn't mind finding a cache of gold, who wouldn't, but that's not all of it and you know it. I want a life for you and Jonah and yes, for me as well, where I don't have to pray for rain or dog someone's trail from one end of the country to the other in order to put meat on the table and clothes on our backs.'

'You were a fine peace officer, Wes, don't belittle your life, there are a lot of people walking around now living their lives in safety because of what you and men like you have done, risked your lives for.'

'I don't exactly see a line of them outside right now offering to dig me a well or pitch feed to our animals.' I tried to hide the anger and bitterness in my voice, but it edged out through my softly spoken words and hung there for us both to see.

'You didn't tell them that was why you were doing what you did. It wasn't why you did it.'

'To hell with it,' was the only thing I could think of to say and the words sounded empty and stupid. I was never one to soak myself in tears of self-pity and standing there in the relative comfort of our home with my lovely wife red-eyed and defiant, the hands of her bare arms held to her hips and my son sleeping contentedly in one of the bedrooms, it would, in any case, have been hard to justify. The hook was set and all I could do was fight the rod, a fruitless venture.

'You have walked the line all your life, Wes, even when things were bad for you in the war. Then, in Colorado and Wyoming, you never once stepped out from behind that badge of yours, never rode a night trail in your life, why start now? Not for us, I won't hear of it.'

I looked at her then, into the sadness of her eyes; fancifully, I thought I saw my father looking out at me echoing her words, and then the moment passed and I sighed and leaned my arm on the shelf above the fireplace easing some of the weight from my sore leg.

'Maybe you are right, Theresa, maybe it is more than that. It was the story, the way it was told to Posy, it sounds so right. So much money waiting there. A gift almost. . . .' My words trailed off as

Ride a Long Shadow

she relaxed and the very slightest hint of a smile teased at the side of her mouth.

'I love you Wesley Harper, rich or poor, drunk or sober, sick or well, but you are wrong in this.' She stood up, a tall, handsome, auburn-haired woman with hazel eyes, erect and straight-backed, as she was at the moment, a cigarette paper's thickness taller than me. 'I can't stop you, wouldn't want to stop you, but remember this, Jonah and I need you, the man, not the money, not a fine ranch and certainly not Comanche gold that in all probability does not even exist. You remember that on cold night-camps or trails that lead you nowhere. Take care of yourself, never cross that line and come back to us soon.'

Theresa was the most practical woman I had ever met. She did not agree with my going or even really fully understand my need to go. That would be asking too much of anyone especially as it was only just then becoming clear to me. However, she did know enough of my feelings and my needs not to fight me. She passed me my glass and raised hers to me.

'Good luck and God speed to you, my love.'

And then she was in my arms and I gathered her up and carried her through to the bedroom, her tears hot on my neck. Behind us I heard the door open quietly as Moke and Posy Tobin came in from the chill evening bringing with them the fragrance of black tobacco and freshly polished leather.

The morning sun was burning the mist from around the dead course of the creek as I pushed the bay clear of the willow trees and looked back towards the ranch house. Smoke was whispering out from the top of the stone stack and Theresa, Jonah and Moke were still standing side by side under the pine archway by the yard entrance straining I knew, as I was, for one last glimpse before I crested the low hill and we were lost to each other for I knew not how long.

I headed the bay westward, waving as I rode by them to the group of Irish drill hands I had hired to sink me three new wells on the property. The wells and their attendant windmills would solve the water problem and the feed I had ordered in from town should keep the cattle alive until rain found its way back to our thirsty valley. Dollar bills bought a great deal of friendship and my neighbour had agreed to supervise the workers and to ensure that the feed I had paid for was duly delivered along with the water. I had no real worries there, in his way he was a decent man trying, as I was, to make a living, to make something of our lives, to fight back against the elements that cared little for the sacrifices made or the hardships endured in order to wrest a living from the capricious land.

Theresa's words rode with me on those three long days and nights as I pushed on at a ground-covering rate heading for the meeting with Posy Tobin. Had I crossed some sort of line? Was I in any danger of crossing over and riding the edge of the nightrider's trail, that dark way I had in the past so doggedly followed, riding hard behind a nickel silver badge with federal ammunition in my Colt. I didn't think so and neither did I believe that Posy was about to cross that line.

THREE

At noon on the fourth day after a cold breakfast of clear stream water and corn dodgers, I broke into the rough country that stretches beyond Del Rio and out into the Chisos Mountains. My plan was to turn north for the Hill Country and the Llano River and a meeting with Tobin at a small settlement adjacent to the abandoned Fort Bowie at the head of the San Saba river. The US Army had quit the fort two summers since, but Tobin said the bluecoats were heading back on account of the Apache running south to the border and then turning again to raid just as soon as they thought the will of Washington had faltered and they were free again to burn and murder as they saw fit. However, Washington was tougher and meaner than even the rugged Apache and a new command was heading west to stop them once and for all time. That, again, was according to Tobin's information. It may have been true or it

Ride a Long Shadow

may have been meant as a comforter to me, an encouragement to follow the golden trail he had so excitedly laid out for me. No man in his right mind would seek out trouble or direct confrontation with the Apache. And this was my thinking as I crossed a trail left by a dozen or so unshod ponies about fifty miles south of Fort Bowie on a hot midday with the dust settling around me like a cloud. I ground-hitched the bay and crawled on hands and knees to a rocky ridge overlooking my back trail, the flat countryside beyond which I had so easily traversed hours earlier. I bellied down on a sunbaked, flat-topped rock and, careful not to allow the bright sun to reflect off their lenses, I adjusted the focal length of my army field-glasses and studied the group of riders behind me.

Coyotero Apache, I guessed, fifteen of them in baggy coats and pants, armed with bows and repeating rifles and leading several spare ponies. Like the animals, they were painted for war, white, black and red streaks on their faces and foreheads. One man was on the ground hunkered down and examining my broken trail and pointing up towards the rocks behind which I hid. One Apache riding a gaunt but sturdy pinto, twisted in his saddle and shook a lance in my direction. Through the glass I looked right back at him. A savage, brown, flat-nosed face, the left cheek heavily scarred, a burn it looked like, and part of his left nostril missing, shaved to the cheek from the tip of the nose to the crease of his upper lip. They milled around some more and the scout remounted and the man with the lance led the band off to the north, heading, I supposed, to the flat canyons into which I would have been riding had I not seen them first. They would ride in a wide loop and either cut my trail to the north or be there ahead of me. Either way it looked like they were hungry for blood and I was on the menu. I slithered back down the slope, cutting my knee even through the thickness of my shotgun chaps. I examined the tear in leather, denim and skin, figured that I could live with it and swung back aboard the bay. The animal, like me, was tired. I guided it back over my own trail to where the Apache had earlier gathered and then followed their trail north for three hours, leaving it where they cut to the east, to supposedly head me off, then I headed due north again.

I rode with great care that afternoon, keeping to the lowland and the sagebrush-covered draws, avoiding the hills and ridges, walking mostly to keep the dust down and to conserve the bay lest we had to make a run for it. I rode on long after dark and finally dry-camped by a worn-out stream bed, protected at my back by a stunted mesquite and to both left and right by rocky high

Ride a Long Shadow

banks. The sky was moonless and black, the faraway stars flickering brightly, lighting the open countryside in a flat white light that shadowed the rocks and granite outcrops making me more nervous than I actually was. The dark of midnight and the Apache. Put those two together with a night bird's call or the wail of a distant coyote and you have one hell of a recipe for a sleepless night. I kept the bay close at hand and slept for five minutes out of every thirty, chasing the chill of the wilderness night away with sips of brandy and mouthfuls of hard corn dodger. By the time the faintest of white lights gilded the eastern horizon, I was back on the bay and running for the San Saba, Fort Bowie and the gold which Posy Tobin had promised awaited us at the end of our particular rainbow.

A settlement was about all it really was. Little more than a trading post. A saloon and a handful of buildings that had sprung up under the protection of the fort and then, when the fort had been abandoned, so too had the settlement. Tobin had been right, both had been reoccupied. A tall, bearded man in a stovepipe hat was sweeping the boarded porch of the store and a fat man in a greasy apron tossed dirty water from a wooden bucket out through the batwing doors of the saloon. There were several weary-looking horses

Ride a Long Shadow

tied to the single hitching rail and a flat-coated grey dog was watching a cat chase a butterfly that had ventured in from the bluebonnets. The flowers set a colourful blue carpet along the bank of the cold-water stream which had been the reason for the choice of the site as a US Army post. The dog cocked open one eye, but seemed too tired to do much about the cat and showed not the slightest interest in me as I rode past him. An American flag hung listlessly from one of the fort's two flagpoles. From the other, the colours of the 6th Cavalry drooped with equal lethargy. The fort's gates were open and sentries posted. The usual raggle-taggle of drifters and transient Indians had set up home just outside the large timber gates and several cooking fires sent grey shafts of smoke straight up into the still morning air.

I rode in through the gates, nodded to the sentry who briefly touched the bill of his campaign hat and waved me on through. I headed directly over to the sutler's store where Posy Tobin sat in a rocker protected from the sun by the store's wooden overhang, drinking coffee from a tin cup.

It was good coffee. After a brief greeting and ensuring the bay's well-being, I sat on the steps and burned my tongue on the drink's sweet, dark, rich heat.

'You're damn near a day late, expected you yesterday afternoon, thought maybe you'd lost your hair,' Tobin grinned, the smile almost cutting his thin face in two and lifting the drooping ends of the long, nicotine-stained moustache.

'I had to make a detour, lost me half a day,' I said, relaxing back into being around people again and not having to constantly look back over my shoulder or to the hidden places at my left or right where ambush could be sprung at any moment.

'Apache?'

'About fifteen of them I would guess. Coyotero probably. They cut my trail about forty miles to the south of here. They carried repeating rifles, Henrys it looked like.'

'That's quite a bunch; better report it in. Colonel Alexander, he's all right, he's old army. He'll listen, it's what he's out here for.'

'Later.'

'Did you get a real close look?'

'Good enough. Man at their head had a bad burn on his face and maybe only half a nose.'

'That's bad news, Wes.' Tobin sucked in his lower lip and glared at me like it was my fault I'd seen an Apache with a split nose.

'That would be Choya, they call him Cut Nose. Ran one time with Santana. Rumour has it Santana's heading this way. I also heard he'd shot himself to death in the Chinati Mountains. Don't know what to believe anymore, but Santana, dead or alive, makes little difference if Choya's out

Ride a Long Shadow

there.'

'I'll go report it in, sounds serious.'

'You do that. I'll organize a meal and some quarters for you for the night. Maybe we'll get drunk before we ride out.' He smiled a cold smile at me.

I gave the corporal orderly my name and told him I wanted to speak with his superior officer. He looked me up and down, no doubt disapproving of my dirty clothes, and went in to see his colonel. He came out moments later and ushered me through the door and into the office of Colonel Tom Alexander, Officer Commanding, Fort Bowie, Texas. I dosed the door behind me and leaned my back on it.

Alexander was a dark-skinned, handsome man with a shock of steel-grey hair covering his head and cut to a slight curl just above his narrow shoulders. His thick moustache was black with a hint of silver encroaching on its neatly trimmed edges. Sharp black eyes stared over a sheaf of papers as he looked me up and down, taking in no doubt, the dust lying on my clothes and grimed into the creases of my unshaved face, the tear in my chaps, the trail dirt on my canvas jacket and the ivory grips on the pistol that sat holstered, butt forward, just below belly button. If he did not approve of what he saw he did not show it; instead, to my complete surprise, he grinned a

Ride a Long Shadow

wide grin, stood up and reached across the table to me, his hand open, waiting for mine to take it. We shook hands and he waved me to the one chair in front of his wide and uncluttered desk. I sat down and wondered what the hell the man was so pleased about.

'I can see you do not remember me, Mr Harper.'

I shook my head searching back to my spell with the Federals during and after the Civil War. The Wilderness, the Rappahannock River, Fredericksburg and later, much later, Washington. There was something about him, but I could not place it, it had all been so long ago, so much had happened and not all of it good. He put me out of my embarrassed misery with a gentle wave of his hand.

'I only met you the two times. I was one of the Old Man's aides, a shavetail second lieutenant then. I was the first to reach you after the assassination attempt that nobody talks about, the one where you took two rounds meant for the Chief.[1] I was right there in the rose garden when you took out the two men tried kill the Old Man. I was with him again when he presented you that silver pistol you are wearing, visiting with you in Armoury Square Hospital in Washington. How's it inscribed, the sentiment?'

---

[1] See *The Shadow Rider*

I didn't speak so he answered his own question.

'"For all my tomorrows, 1872". It's a pre-production model Colt .45 as I remember it.' He was smiling broadly then. 'Hell, I even cut the papers got you out of the Colorado State Prison and back on a marshal's payroll.'

I stared at him dead-eyed. It was something I had sworn never to talk about. My days as a presidential bodyguard, the attempt on Grant's life, my part in his salvation.

'It's OK, Mr Harper, I know it's not to be talked about, but I just wanted you to know where we had met. I've thought about you often, wondered what happened to you. Last I heard you were in Wyoming, got yourself married. I still write to the Old Man, he'll be tickled pink to know how dirty you are.' He laughed and I joined him. He called for a bottle and dismissed the orderly. 'We'll drink to old times and say no more about that particular day, fair enough?'

'Fair enough, Colonel, but when you do write to the Old Man, please give him my fondest wishes, and call me Wes, my army days are long behind me.'

'You can count on it, Wes. Now what are you doing way out here, I don't see a badge on your vest?'

I sipped at the whiskey. 'I'm kind of retired, Colonel, I was hoping to do a little prospecting up in the Hill Country with an old friend, see if we could find anything the Comanche or the Spanish may have left behind.'

He stared at me, a twinkle flashing in his dark eyes. 'Bowie's gold? Hell, don't tell me the Shadow Rider's gone and bought himself a fifty-year-old treasure map, those things are a dime a dozen out here.'

'Shadow Rider?'

'It's what they call you now, isn't it?'

'Didn't expect to hear it is all. Washington yes, but not out here, it has kind of a different meaning among Westerners.'

'Oh?' He raised his bushy eyebrows at me.

'Yes, it's latched on to a man who rides the trail admiring his own shadow.'

He laughed again. 'Not the way I heard it was tagged on to you. Coming out of the shadows was how I heard it, smoking, bringing your man back on a saddle one way or another, head up or head down.'

'That was a long time ago and no, I haven't bought a map, we're just going to kick some rocks around, see what we find.' I don't think that he believed me but was far too much of an officer and a gentleman to show it.

'None of my business anyway, the Apache are my worry,' he said quietly, changing the subject and the mood of the meeting. 'I've got a wildfire of

Ride a Long Shadow

trouble all around me and only a bucket of troopers to quell it with. You see anything I should know about on your ride in?'

'Was why I visited with you, Colonel. Forty miles or so to the south of here I ran across a mounted war party, Coyotero they looked like, but to tell the truth I didn't care to get that close to them to be certain of that. Some of them were sporting Henry rifles and from the description of their leader I gave my partner, he figures him to be Choya. I thought you should know about that.'

'Choya!' he shouted back at me. 'Great goddamn, how many with him?' He leaned across the desk towards me, old times and new whiskey forgotten.

'Fifteen I saw, maybe a couple of outriders I missed.'

'Big band, eh? Coyotero you think?'

I nodded.

'That would be right if Choya is leading them, but it's also odd, the Coyotero run further to the north and west of here, wonder why they headed out this way.'

'Meet up with Santana maybe if what they say about him springing from Huntsville is true.'

'That part's true enough, although I would have thought he would have run for the border, hit back from there maybe, not up here.'

'No telling what an Apache will do especially

with anger in his heart.'

'Henry rifles, that's also bad news. What kind of man would sell an Indian a repeating rifle?'

'What kind of man would send an Apache to the East to grow corn and hope that he would stay there?' I did not hide my feelings behind the words. In many ways the white man was getting all that he asked for from the Apache. The Plains Indians may have succumbed following the aftermath of the big fight with Custer up on the Greasy Grass River, had the fight kicked out of them by the army, the settlers and the hunters who slew the buffalo and made them dependent on the whites for food and shelter. Not the Apache though. This was rugged country, a long ride between homesteads and settlements, the army couldn't cover it and the Apache knew that, took full advantage of it. Hit and run. The whites were reaping the whirlwind of their own making.

Alexander leaned back in his chair and wrapped his hands behind his head seeming at one and the same time to sense my hostility and to sympathize with it.

'The army doesn't make the policy out here, Wes, we just do our best to enforce it and so far this year it has cost the lives of twenty-five good men from this fort alone, including my second-in-command. I'm hoping for replacements and the word is that this time we'll chase them clear across the border if we have to.'

'And kill them there.'

'Not if they come back peacefully.'

'I don't see that happening, Colonel.' I got to my feet and set the empty glass on his desk. 'Thanks for the drink. It was good to see you, to remember you. I believe I have you now; sorry it took so long and for the rough edge of my tongue, old age and meanness I guess.' I smiled with the words wanting to show him there were no ill feelings between the two of us. I think he understood and held out his hand to me again.

'We could use some extra white scouts, Wes. You and your partner have been around, I have less than thirty mounted here.' He let the words hang there.

I shook his hand firmly and released it, matching his crafty smile with one of my own. 'Not this trip, Soldier, but thanks for asking.'

Outside, the afternoon sun was low in the west, a washed-out orange-red ball shimmering in the heat-haze of a cloudless sky. The parade ground was freshly raked and a pile of steaming horse manure scented the cooling air. A horse called from the stables and its call was answered by another. Soldiers passed me by, some looking curiously at my dusty clothes and behind me to where Alexander stood leaning against the door jamb. They saluted and I assume he responded, the men, like the horses, needing to communicate. I walked across the square to where Tobin was still seated in the rocker, a corncob pipe between his thin lips.

'I'm about ready for that food you promised me and the drink you hinted at, Posy.'

'I'm not eating with you less'n you wash some of the stink off you. I got you a room out back of the sutler's and hot water laid on. What did the general have to say about Choya?'

'He wasn't too happy with the news, wants to sign us up.'

Tobin laughed. 'We got our own work to do. Murchison and the Coys were holed up in a box canyon five miles to the north of here until early this morning. They was joined there by three other mean-looking sons of bitches and a Mex woman they probably stole. The whole bunch of them headed north at sun-up, leading a string of mules, they seemed to know where they were going.'

'They leave a clear enough trail?'

'That many riders will, one both of us could follow. Perhaps we'll give the hard drinking a miss tonight. I do believe Choya, Murchison, the Coys and the rest of them deserve our undivided attention.'

FOUR

The bluebonnets and cottonwoods of the river valley quickly gave way to sagebrush, mesquite and scrub as we took to the higher ground. The bay seemed refreshed after a night's rest and, I supposed fancifully, an evening's conversation with a cavalry officer's chestnut mount with whom he had shared a stall. Tobin rode tall in the saddle pushing the big sorrel on, eager to be on the trail; for my part, I had failed to take my own advice and had joined Alexander for an after supper drink and an unaccustomed cigar. We had talked about the old, sometimes better days, and of mutual comrades long since dead. Soldiers in arms who had died by our sides on one bloody battlefield or another. It was immortality of a sort for those dead comrades, ten years on and still they lived in our slightly inebriated thoughts as if it were only yesterday that we saw them stagger and fall. It was incredible that, although we had

Ride a Long Shadow

only met twice, our paths had crossed within yards or a mile or two so many times. Now my head hurt considerably and my tongue felt like a lump of untanned leather in my mouth, but the bay had an easy step, seldom stumbled and rarely bucked and I hung on as the headache dwindled, diluted with cold drinking water and the pleasurable call of a hunting red-tailed hawk. It was a beautiful morning and my full attention was not required, Murchison's party left a trail a one-eyed man could have followed.

The party ahead of us moved very slowly, doubling back here and there searching the draws and gullies, covering only five miles in the whole of the dusty day. That first night we dry camped within sight of their campfire, it glowed and sparked like a diamond in the night and we both wondered at their casualness given the fact that Choya was in the area. Tobin was curiously taciturn and had been since we had ridden out of Fort Bowie. It was as if some new energy had taken him over, he was a driven man on the edge of something I did not quite fully understand. I asked him about the lack of care shown by our quarry, but he was dismissive of my concern, offering only that they may have felt so well armed and capable of producing enough firepower for anything or anyone they came up against. I didn't argue the matter. We had a formidable

Ride a Long Shadow

array of weapons of our own. Apart from the dynamite packed along with the bulk of our provisions on the back of a burro, we each carried two sidearms and a rifle or carbine. Should any close in-fighting be called for, I had purchased a sawn-off Greener from the sutler together with a box of unidentified orange-coloured cartridges. They rattled like double-ought buck and the contents felt solid and comforting.

The following morning we risked a small fire ourselves, drank down hot coffee and ate fried eggs to drive out the invasive cold of the night. Both of my legs hurt, the cold nagged at them where the puckered scars glowed white beneath my jeans from a round fired at me by the late Arkansas Bob Deacon. He had been the last man I had killed while wearing a federal badge and the surprise in his face concentrated in the sharpness of his dead eyes, stared out from the breakfast fire at me and I shivered.

'Not coming down with something are you, Wes?' Tobin asked. He was ready to ride while I was still finishing my breakfast.

I ignored him, finished my coffee, cleaned the cup and plate in the dust and stowed the gear in one of the burro's leather panniers. Then mounted and with Tobin on point, we headed for Murchison's camp and the continuing trail that would, we believed, lead us on to Bowie's gold.

Ride a Long Shadow

*

The Mexican girl looked about done in when we found her at the campsite earlier vacated by the outlaws. She was suspended from the strong grey branch of a cottonwood, her wrists bloody from the weight dragged down and into them by the wet leather thongs used to tie her there. She was half-naked, her cotton skirt and blouse ripped open revealing great bruises on her small breasts and flat stomach. The outsides of her thighs were bloody and her naked, dirty feet were cut and dangling inches above the rocky ground. She had been a pretty woman at one time, *guapa*, pretty and sexy, although that was hard to see now. Her lips were split, her nose bleeding and one eye was completely closed. Tobin rode right on by her, but the bay shied when she moaned and I reined the animal in and called after him that I was going to cut her down. He turned back agitated at the delay.

'She's finished, man, leave her and let's be moving on.'

'I can't do that, Posy,' I said. 'You keep the trail, I'll check her out and catch you up later.'

He stared down at me as I dismounted and walked towards the pitiful ragged, hanging figure, my knife in my hand.

'You're getting to be an old woman, Wes; yesterday you damn near fell off your horse from the drink and today you want to play Samaritan to a half-dead Mex. Suit yourself though. I'll leave a clear enough trail for you to follow and double back if there is trouble. Watch your back, don't lose the mule and don't take all day about this.'

He turned and touched his horse with the spur before I could answer, if answer I was going to. I cut her down as gently as I could and, followed by the bay, carried her to the narrow stream that rattled down from the high ground above. I stripped off her ragged and bloody clothes and washed her, taking great care where the bruising gave way to torn flesh. I dressed the open wounds on her wrists, got some whiskey and water down her and covered her with my blanket. Her eyes had opened from time to time during my ministrations and I had tried to impress upon her that I was a friend, that I meant her no harm. If she understood me she gave no sign of that fact. I did all that I could for her then I pulled my hat low, rested my back against a mossy rock and waited for her to sleep off some of the pain.

She awoke a little after noon, stared at me, gave a startled whimper and struggled to get to her feet. I moved towards her making calming sounds with my voice, like a man might do to a fretful horse. I held my hands palms outwards and she allowed me to touch her and settle her

Ride a Long Shadow

back down. She looked out at me from her one good eye. Fear was there and panic, too, a hopelessness that was probably part of her life long before the Murchison gang had abused her. I smiled and dug into my vest pocket bringing out the US marshal badge I always carried with me. It was solid silver, fashioned from the back-plate of my father's pocket watch by a Wyoming craftsman. It seemed to glow in the hot sunlight and she stared at it and relaxed back against the rock. Authority. She recognized and understood authority whether it was from a uniform or a silver-encircled star.

'You are sheriff?' Her voice was weak, the English halting, but she had been able to understand me, yet even through the pain and the fear she had not revealed that fact lest it went against her.

'I was once a US marshal, still am in some places, not out here though.' I could see she did not believe me.

'You are lawman, you are going to kill those men who did this to me.'

'I'm following them, yes, but only because they have something I want and yes, I will kill them if I have to.'

The words frightened me. Kill them? Shoot them down for the map and the gold? Was that what I was doing out here. Arrest them, relieve them of the map, take them in on whatever warrant they were under, yes, but kill them for the gold? I thought of the fire in Tobin's eyes the day he had told me about the lost mine and wondered if it was now burning in my own. I blinked the thought away.

'Did they rape you?' I asked gently, aware of the anger hidden in the cloak of my words.

'No. Three men, they stole me from my village many weeks ago and they did not use me. They believed I was worth money. I worked hard for them dirty gringos but they did not touch me.'

'Who did this to you then?'

'He did this, the one they call Murchison. He did not take me like a man will sometimes take a woman, in heat, that is not his way. He beat me and enjoyed it, and there was no need for that, no call for him to hurt me, I did not fight with him.'

'The man who hurt you, I know of him.'

'He is not a man, he is not even a cur dog, he is Devil's animal.'

I climbed to my feet and passed the canteen to her. 'We'll take care of it when we need to.'

'We?'

'My partner is following them and' – I glanced over my shoulder to where smoke drifted up from a distant, grey, sagebrush-covered hill – 'I do believe the Apache are following us. Time to move on, girl, you up for that?'

Ride a Long Shadow

She sipped from the canteen and handed it back to me. '*Gracias, hombre.* My name is Maria, I am called after the blessed virgin.'

'My name is Harper and the man I am with is called Tobin, we will take care of you, do our best to get you back to your people.'

'It is a long way from here.' She looked down at the blanket and over at the rags of her own bloody garments. 'I have no clothes to wear.'

I fished my spare pair of Levi's and a red flannel undershirt out of the pack and tossed them to her. While she was getting them on, I slit the centre of my extra blanket and watched as she settled it poncho-like over her narrow shoulders.

'They're a mite big but you look OK. We'll win you a hat from somewheres later on, in the meantime, wrap this kerchief around your head. It's time to go.'

I pulled her slight weight up behind me and, leading the burro, set out after Tobin, guessing at his anger when he saw that I had the woman with me and dismissing the thought with a smile. Her company might make a pleasant change from his smouldering silence.

We caught up with Tobin in the red-skied moments just before sunset. The western horizon was splashed a violent red, the colour dripped from the flattened bottom of the setting sun like molten steel, sending purple shadows racing across the landscape towards us. He stepped out from behind a high granite boulder, leading his horse, his rifle cocked and in the crook of his arm. He gave me the barest of glances and stared up at the woman. Still without looking directly at me he said quietly, 'Jesus Christ, Wes, but you are one goddamned soft-hearted son of a bitch who's going to get us both killed.'

I swung down from the bay and left the woman sitting there. 'You are one profane man, Posy, but I'll do my best to keep you out of Heaven or Hell for a while yet. As for the woman, there is nothing to discuss. She rides with us or I take her back to Bowie now, no way can we leave her here with Choya riding the canyons.'

'She's your problem then; see to it she doesn't get in our way. She does, I'll kill her.' Then as if he had just been passing the time of day with me, and before I could challenge his brutal words, he changed the subject, his voice low, his attention fully with me. 'They moved into a deep box canyon a couple of hours ago. I figured they'd made a bad mistake and would be riding right back out, but they kept on going in. It's about two miles to the west of here and the trail is more difficult to follow was why I rode back to meet you. A stream runs through it and there is grass and scrub oak. Could be an old camp of some kind in there or it

Ride a Long Shadow

could be we reached trail's end. Then again, it could be both. Come morning we'll know for sure.' Again the fire burned in his eyes and again I was not sure if it came from within or if it was simply a reflected light from the setting sun.

'You see the smoke?' I asked, knowing that he would not have missed it.

'Sure, and there is more ahead of us. Two parties powwowing maybe, or the one big party split into two groups. What do you think?'

'It doesn't matter much which way it is, there are too many of them for us to take on, let's hope they keep clear. We making camp here?'

He looked around him. 'There's a cave at the back of this big ol' rock, stinks of cat, but I think he's long gone. We could have us a small fire and some hot coffee. Yes, this is good a place as any I would guess.'

He worked his horse back to the big rock and I followed him, leading the bay and the woman whose life now seemed to be my absolute responsibility, for I did not doubt that Posy would make good his threat if needs must. I wondered, too, if that went for me as well should I get in between him and the gold.

That night after supper, I carefully stripped and cleaned the silver-plated Colt and tended to the army issue, long-barrelled Colt I carried in my

Ride a Long Shadow

saddle-bag. I paid just as much attention to my carbine and to the twelve gauge then, secretively, during my spell at night-watch and long after Posy Tobin had snored his way into a restless sleep, I cleaned the .41 calibre derringer I sometimes packed, and slipped the ugly little two-shot pistol into the soft lining of my right boot.

FIVE

I asked Posy if he had a plan, saying that I believed it a good thing to have a plan to work to. He smiled his narrow smile and told me that I worried too much and that until we actually knew what we were up against we had best wing it. I pointed out to him that we did have a fair idea as to just what we were up against – six gunfighters backed up to a wall and seemingly half of the Apache nation on our trail. He listened and asked me if I had a plan of my own and I told him I damned well did have and it didn't involve riding blindly into a box canyon with Choya sitting on the only way out.

'So what do you suggest, Shadow Rider?' He smiled when he said it, but the inference was plain. I ignored that part of it, but answered his question anyway.

'I'm going to scout these hills this morning, be sure just what is at our back. Fifteen Apache or fifty makes one hell of a difference as to whether or not I ride into that box canyon with you. Gold or no gold, if there is no way out of there then it makes little difference. I'd as soon die a poor man late as a rich man early.'

'You going soft on me, Wes?'

'No, I'm trying to keep us both alive for a little longer is all.'

'You taking her on this expedition with you?'

'No, I'm leaving her here in your care, Posy.' Then I let my own voice harden as his had the previous evening. 'And if anything happens to her I'll damned well hold you responsible for it.'

He grinned that dead smile at me, his black eyes shining. 'Whatever you say. Maybe it would be best at that if she stayed here in the cave. While you scout the hills I'll check on our friends in the canyon. Meet you back here at noon and make the goddamned plan you hanker after. Suit you?'

I nodded, smiled and ran my hand scratchily across the stubble of my beard. 'Sure, they're not going anywheres, are they.'

It wasn't a question and he did not treat it as one.

I explained to Maria about the Apache and our need for concealment. I reassured her that she was in no real danger just so long as she remained hidden and told her we would be back before

Ride a Long Shadow

midday. Then, making sure she knew just how to use it and, I must admit, against my own better judgement and in defiance of Tobin, I left her the shotgun and the box of shells. For no real reason that I could think of, I waited until he was clear of the cave and out of sight on the lower rim of the canyon before setting off on my own uncertain trail.

The bay was a sure-footed animal and we covered the rocky ground easily. I cut several sign of unshod ponies and once, close to mid-morning, I crossed the trail of a single rider. On a whim, I followed the lone horseman on to the bottomland and through a small grove of cottonwoods and *piñon*. There was water there, I could smell it and so could the bay. He pricked his ears and moved a little more quickly to where a tree-shrouded draw ran due west along the foot of the granite hill and the mountain lion cave somewhere above me. Dismounting and tying off the bay, I crawled forward on foot to where I could get a clear view of the open country beyond the trees. A wide creek ran shallow through a rocky gorge and, by a bend, two Coyotero sat cross-legged on a large flat rock, their backs to me. Their hobbled ponies munched at the bunch grass that ranged the banks of the stream and insects buzzed over the bluebonnets and Indian paintbrush that covered the high grassy banks of the creek. One of the Apache

Ride a Long Shadow

grunted and pointed to the south, the view hidden from me by a rise in the ground but clearly visible to them from their higher viewpoint. I got to my knees and then carefully, to my feet. My heart thundered and my face flushed with fear at what I saw and, instinctively, I ducked back down.

When I had remarked to Tobin that there was a considerable difference between fifteen and fifty I had been exaggerating the higher number. Apache did not move in those kinds of numbers anymore, certainly not unless you counted woman, old people and children. Above the borderline they had been harassed and hacked at by the Rangers and the US Army resulting in many spending time on reservations or in prison, the remainder broken down into small war parties who marauded more than they fought pitched battles. Twenty-five would have been the maximum I would have expected to see and I guess that would have been the thinking of the army as well. Certainly, Alexander had thought Choya's band of fifteen was a high number and handful enough for his small garrison. Someone was in for a shock. Riding across that open land and heading my way, still several miles off, was a mounted band of fighting men numbering upwards of ninety to a hundred Apache. An amalgamation I supposed, of Coyotero, Kiowa and Chiricahua. A formidable force and one that was

Ride a Long Shadow

likely to be headed for Fort Bowie as well as anywhere.

I drank from my canteen and considered my options. I had told Tobin that I would be back by noon, but that was now out of the question. I had to hold my ground and in some way determine the direction the Apache would take and when they would do it. Certainly at that moment they were headed for the watering place and the shelter of the trees and away from the general direction of Bowie which lay, by my reckoning, fifteen miles to the west. If I stayed and watched, as I felt I should, what would Tobin's reaction be, would he wait for my return or try for the gold, if indeed the gold were there, on his own? Would he assume I had been taken by the Coyotero and write me off and in so doing, write the woman off as well? No way the Apache were going to ride up and tell me their plans so it was a purely a matter of observation and a careful evaluation of what I saw. This was not new territory for me. I had scouted for both Grant and Sheridan as they marched through the Shenandoah Valley and I had been good at my job. Younger too. I rubbed at my left leg which had begun to ache the moment I saw the Apache riding across the open countryside. Some men's bunions play up when it is going to rain, another man I knew got earache before a thunderstorm burst upon him, but me, my leg

Ride a Long Shadow

hurts like all hell when I think I'm about to be killed.

I slithered quietly back to the bay and took my field-glasses from their case around the saddle horn and, returning to my vantage point, I set the glass on the oncoming riders. Choya at their head, no doubt about it. He carried a lance and I could see a repeating rifle hanging by a leather strap across his broad shoulders. Many of the men carried Henrys, although a few carried older weapons, Springfields and even a muzzle loader or two were mixed in with those who carried spear and bow. All were painted for war. This was no marauding hit-and-run band; out there, as if riding directly at me, was a formidable army of some of the hardest and toughest fighting men in the world. For just one moment I wished the desk-bound bureaucrats in Washington with their tightwad politician bosses who kept the army underfunded and, some would say, undermanned, could feel both the fear and the exhilaration I felt at that moment.

I stayed throughout that afternoon and long into the evening before, with some reluctance, vacating my safe hiding place at first light, feeling fairly certain that there was no immediate haste to head back for the fort and report my sighting of Choya's heavily armed and numerous band. Upon arrival at the creek, the war party had quite unhurriedly set up a semi-permanent camp, built fires and crude lodges, enough to give shelter from the fierce sun or from the rain promised by a dark anvil-shaped gathering of clouds in the hills above and behind me. They would make their medicine for a day or two and then, I was certain of it, they would ride the long half-day's hard ride for the decimated unsuspecting fort and attempt to do for the Western Apache what Sitting Bull and Crazy Horse had done for the Sioux and the Northern Cheyenne. A big victory would be of benefit to them either for negotiating a lasting and just peace or for the continued bloody war. At least, I had no doubt that that was how Choya saw it. In reality it would be different. Destruction of Fort Bowie and the wiping out of part of the 6th Cavalry would result in the same level of devastating retribution wrought upon the Sioux following Custer's massive defeat in the Dakotas. I had no wish for that to happen either to the Apache, whose cause I had some sympathy with, or to Alexander and the dusty, blue-shirted soldiers under his sure command.

A misty rain blew down from the mountains and soaked the bay and me. My duster was already wet and heavy on my shoulders when the mist turned into a steady downpour and the dry creek beds I had crossed earlier with ease, roared and rattled their way downwards giving us pause

Ride a Long Shadow

for thought several times before we crossed over or rode through them. Thunder lanced at the hillside, stabbing at it, and once, not a hundred yards from where I sheltered in the lee of a rocky overhang, a great crackling tongue of yellow forked down and into a tall pine tree, splitting it and firing it at the same time. The downpour swiftly quenched the blue flame, but the damp stink of burned woodsmoke and scorched air filled my nostrils with their bitter tang. We pushed quickly on and upwards, the bay rolling its eyes, and mine, half closed against the rain and the drip from my hat brim, casting left and right for a new shelter I could not find. The lightning visited us once more and then, as quickly as it had appeared, the storm moved off to the west and I breathed easier, relaxed a little into the ride and learned to live with the constant trickle of cold water running down the back of my neck.

SIX

'Where the blue blazes have you been?' Tobin barked at me, stepping out of the evening shadows, his rifle pointed at my belly, as the bay broke into the dark clearing in front of the cave.

I stared down at him. 'And what the hell happened to "Welcome back, Wes, glad the Apache didn't stake your ass out over a slow fire". What the goddamned kind of welcome back is this?'

He relaxed, lowered the rifle, offered a strained grin and took the bay's rein as I squelched down from the wet saddle. 'Sorry, man, got the night creeps is all. Damned coyote that might not be a coyote keeps howling and that miserable Mex woman won't take her good eye off me or put that scatter-gun down and I do swear that most of the time it's pointed in my direction. Hell, glad you made it back in one piece, but what the hell kept you anyway?'

'Get me some hot coffee on while I take care of

my horse, we need to talk.'

Later, with the bay alongside Tobin's mount and the burro in back of the cave, we sat by a small fire at the high entrance drinking coffee and eating beans and biscuits. Maria had shown an obvious relief at my return, seeing me as her protector from the Murchison gang, the Apache and now, I supposed, Posy Tobin.

'You going to keep me waiting all night, man?' Tobin asked, scraping the juice from his plate into the sizzling fire and squatting back down opposite me, our eyes meeting over the low flames.

I set my own plate down and wrapped my hands around the warm tin cup of coffee. 'You may not believe it – I had a hard enough job convincing myself – but old Choya's got himself together a regular army. A hundred or more, mixed, Kiowa, Coyotero and some Chiricahua, all bucks, no old folks or kids in sight. And they're painted for war.'

Tobin thought about it for a long minute before speaking. 'A hundred you say, and where was this?'

'In the flatlands, about ten miles south from here straight down, maybe fifteen from the fort.'

'The fort? Why do you say the fort?'

'Because that's where I believe they're headed once they have made enough strong medicine. A day or two, three at the most.'

'Why are you so sure of that?'

Ride a Long Shadow

'Nowhere else for them to go, Posy. A surprise attack from a big band like that would overrun the settlement and Fort Bowie with it. They wouldn't stand a chance.'

His voice dropped a tone. 'That's a damned shame.'

'What do you mean, a damned shame?'

'All of those soldier boys and Alexander, he seemed OK for an officer.'

'What's your point?' I asked quietly, staring through the shimmering heat of the fire at him, again noting the red of his eyes, glowing like a coyote frozen in the firelight, wild eyes, a fiery pink.

'Not a damned thing we can do about it; there's only the two of us, two guns wouldn't make that much of a difference one way or the other.'

'Hell,' I said, getting to my feet, raising my voice a little. 'It isn't a matter of two guns, if the garrison were ready for them it would make one hell of a difference, maybe all of the difference. Somebody's got to ride back and warn Alexander and before too long.'

Tobin got to his feet and faced me. He was taller than me, but I held the higher ground inside the cave's mouth. 'We're too close, leave those goddamned murdering bastards now and they'll run with the money, they been digging all day for Christ's sake, they must be so damned close to the gold now. They may have it already for all we know.'

'You want to go for the gold and leave the fort to go to hell, is that what you're telling me here, Posy?'

He thought about it for a moment or two and relaxed back into his old self, shrugging his shoulders, smiling a tired smile. There was no humour in it though and I did not relax my guard in any way.

'Way I see it, Wes, we can do both. You say the Apache will make medicine for a couple of days, then we're home and dry. In the morning we take the gold from Murchison and the next day one of us stays with the mules while the other rides for the fort. It makes a lot of sense. A whole lot more savvy than both of us running for Bowie now.'

'Just like that?' I matched his smile. 'We go in and take the gold and they give it to us and wish us a great day in the morning.'

'No not just like that.' He sat back down, but I remained standing. 'Not just like that at all. We'll have to kill them for sure, leastwise, some of them.'

'Kill them? Bushwhack them you mean?'

'Don't go all the way soft on me, Wes, you knew all along it would come to that one way or another. They're all hired guns, killers, horsethieves, rapists.' He nodded to the silent Maria who was obviously having difficulty in following most of our conversation. 'Wanted men with paper on them from every whichway.'

I sighed and sat back down, my legs creaking with the motion. He was right, of course; I had known and it would do no good to pretend otherwise. 'If it can be done in a day, then I'll ride with you, Posy, it was why I came and I do need my share of the gold and that's the truth. We give them a fair chance to surrender though and whatever happens after that is down to them. Alexander has to be warned so I'm telling you here and now, if things go bad in there or it gets to be a stand-off, then I'll cut and run. That's the best I can say.'

'It's good enough, Wes, we have a deal on the table now and all we need is that goddamned plan of yours.'

I smiled at him. 'We do, don't we? Tell me the layout, what you've seen in there and let's get her done.'

The box canyon was much as Tobin had described it to me, drawn in the soft sand of the cave's mouth, etched with a stick by the dying light of our campfire. Neither of us had slept much after that and the first shaft of morning light filtering into our refuge was a welcome sight. We had eaten a cold breakfast washed down with canteen water and then, leaving Maria to watch over our gear and the burro, we quickly covered the two miles to the canyon's mouth.

Once it had been a wide-mouthed canyon with hard-running water, scrub oaks, grass and shade from the noon sun, a good place to corral cattle or horses, and there was evidence of that with split pine and larch rails rotting in the ground, showing it may well have been used for just such a purpose. That would have had been some time ago though. Now it was mostly blocked with fallen rock and rubble, either set there deliberately or fallen there with the passing of time. The rocky Western landscape changes rapidly and even the best memory or the clearest drawn map will confound the individual with the passing of the years. The combination of the rain and the wind is more than a match for the traveller who relies on an isolated landmark as his way of orientation. No wonder it had taken them so long to identify the canyon from the map they carried, a map that would have been drawn fifty years before they had killed for it.

There was no mistaking it, it was there in front of us and we went for it, eagerly.

It was very narrow with barely enough room to get the horses inside of the entrance, but we managed it, dismounting just inside, tying the animals off to the remains of an old mine prop

Ride a Long Shadow

that slanted endwise out of the rocks. I carried the shotgun as well as my pistol, but Posy had declined any weapon other than his knife and sidearm. We removed our spurs and wrapped our boots with rags before continuing up the narrow defile, crossing and recrossing the fast running but shallow water where the track faded and switched from bank to bank. I was the first to smell the cigarette smoke and cautioned Tobin ahead with great care. We paused at a sharp bend in the trail and poked our heads gently around the corner. A scarecrow of a man was sitting on a flat rock smoking a thin quirly. He was shaggy of hair and beard, slight of build, around forty years old, dressed in rags and muddy lace-up town boots. He was half-turned away from us, more interested in what was going on behind him than who might be coming up the back trail. He wore a belt gun in an army flap holster and an old Sharps buffalo gun was propped against the granite at his feet. We pulled back out of sight and Tobin nodded, got down on all fours and vanished around the corner. I gave him a minute and then peered after him. I was just in time to see him grab the man from behind and to catch the flash of steel as he drove his knife into the man's back cutting sideways and slicing through the spinal cord. The man sagged in his arms and Tobin hoisted him back on to the rock, set his battered hat straight and leaned him that way with his back to the interior of the canyon, for all the world like he was still sitting there, doing his guard duty.

I reached Tobin just as he was wiping the blade of his knife on the man's pants leg. 'You had to kill him?' It was a foolish question and he ignored it motioning instead to the activity along and slightly below us.

Jim Bowie's Lost Mine, *Los Almagres*, the rainbow's end.

SEVEN

Rafe Murchison was easily recognizable from the flyers I had seen in the post office back at Uvaldi. Once a lawman, always a lawman and I never visited the place without noting the faces staring dead eyed out of the paper at me, wanted men by both state and federal authorities. A tall man in tailored black pants and shirt, dusty now but quality nevertheless. He wore a pointed black Montana Peak over long black hair; sideways on, his nose was big and hawk-like, the hook over a drooping black moustache. His holstered pistol was tied down just above his bent knee as he sat on an old stump out back of a derelict cabin, watching the backbreaking activities of the four men working rotting canvas bags out into the sunlight from the mine's entrance, tipping the bars – gold and silver – into darkly tanned leather panniers. There were five of the big bags and one smaller one close by to Murchison's black-booted foot. The tall man fired a cigar and said something to the nearest figure, a pasty-faced, rail-thin youngster who carried a bag over to him and watched while he examined the contents before dumping them into the small pannier. The youngster returned to his work and was joined by another man, an older man, kin he looked like, coming out from the mine. They talked for a moment or two and then the younger one returned to the mine and the second man joined Murchison, borrowed a match from him, struck it on his pants leg and fired a half-smoked cheroot. Tobin whispered that they were the Coy brothers, bad medicine from the Big Thicket and that it was about time they had some law around here. He fished in his pocket and brought out his Ranger badge, a silver star set in a circle, the badge struck from a Mexican five peso coin.

'I kept it when I resigned, thought it might come in handy some day; looks like today's the day, it'll get their attention.' He was a happy man.

We watched for a while longer formulating some sort of action that would offer the least risk to us. Certainly we wanted all five men out in the open, getting the drop on them might not be too hard if they were all outside, but one man in the mine could cause us a real problem. We moved closer, keeping low. Even so, I don't think it would really have mattered too much if we had been whistling 'Dixie', the men were so wrapped up in their new-found wealth as to be all but oblivious to our approach. Good luck for them it was us and not the Apache, I thought to myself, and then, seeing the cold, deadly light in Posy Tobin's eyes, I began to wonder if it mattered that much either way.

It seemed their work was about done when the three men emerged from the mine. The leading two were similar in appearance to the one whose life Tobin had taken with the keen edge of his knife, and behind them, the younger Coy tossed a shovel he had been carrying back into the darkness. Murchison slid off the stump and walked over to the bank opposite the entrance and leaned on a lightning-struck oak that loomed low over the clearing. We had split up on our final approach and I was close enough to hear him as he addressed the four outlaws.

'We're about done here I guess. Luke, you bring up the mules and you and Matt pack them and make sure it's the best tying down you ever done.' He grinned and the two Coys let out Rebel yells that startled a flock of doves from out of the high rocks above our heads. 'Tom, you and Leroy clear up back there, take a stick of dynamite back in the mine, a hundred yards or so, and blow the roof, if there is anything left back in there then let it stay, we got ours.'

Ride a Long Shadow

'Could be it isn't all yours, Rafe,' Tobin said conversationally, stepping out from behind the oak and pointing his pistol at the startled group. The man called Leroy twitched his fingers claw-like over his holstered pistol and Tobin moved his own piece on to the man. 'I wouldn't want you to do that.'

The words were flat and deadly and the man froze raising his hands as Murchison, the Coys and the other man had done.

'What the hell are you doing way out here, Tobin?' Murchison asked the question casually, unhurried and seemingly unperturbed by the man's sudden appearance at his very moment of triumph. For my part, still hidden in the rocks behind them, I was surprised, having had no idea that the two men knew each other. Tobin hadn't mentioned it to me and I wondered if there was anything else he had forgotten to tell me along the way.

'Just my job, Rafe. Now, reach across with your left hands and unbuckle your gunbelts, slow and easy. You,' he stabbed the gun at the younger Coy, 'Luke, you being a lefty and all, use your right hand. Do it.'

Nobody moved.

Tobin moved the muzzle of his pistol from Murchison to the man named Tom and capped the round under the hammer. The pistol cracked loud

Ride a Long Shadow

in the confined space, bounced and racketed off of the walls as the bullet tore into the man's chest, turning him around, sending him to Hell face down in the clearwater stream. Blood welled out of the exit wound in the back of the dirty plaid shirt and the man coughed a clutch of red bubbles once, and died there.

'I don't want to have to tell you again,' Tobin said quietly, and four gunbelts hit the dirt. 'I gave him the chance I promised you. Wes.' He threw the word across the clearing at me.

I chose that moment to step clear of the crumbling shack, the shotgun at the ready, both hammers on full cock, not wanting to use it and hoping my appearance would dissuade Tobin from gunning down any more of them. There was a madness in his eyes, I caught it and so did the imperturbably cool Murchison. 'Another Ranger?' he said, his dead voice matching that of Tobin's. 'How many men you got out there with you, Posy?'

Again the familiarity.

'Enough, Rafe, enough for scum like you and the Coy boys here. Now, get down and sit on your hands and shut up while I make up my mind whether or not to kill you.'

The men did as they were told, the older Coy cussing, but the rest doing it quietly, not certain if Tobin was serious about killing them in cold blood as well. I moved past the sitting men to the entrance of the cave, curiosity getting the better of me and a need to see the interior of a gold-mine long since relegated to part of Western myth, no more real than Flint's Treasure or the fabled lost wealth of the Incas. It was pretty insignificant as real-life myths go. Dirt and rock, rotten timbers busted props and what looked like piles of rags and sticks which, upon closer examination, revealed themselves to be two raggedy buckskin-clothed skeletons.

I turned back to where Murchison was sitting on his hands, 'You weren't the first to find it then, seems like someone else got here before you.'

'Oh, I believe we were.' He smiled up at me as if we were engaged in pleasant after-dinner conversation and there wasn't a dead man face down in the creek. 'They were Comanche by the cut of their clothes; old Jim Bowie took 'em out I would guess. He seems to have left in hurry else he would have sealed off the whole canyon. It didn't even take us a day to clear the mine entrance.'

'Watch them, Wes, while I take a looksee just how rich we are.' Tobin walked over to one of the panniers, looked inside and gave a long low whistle. He moved to the smaller bag, knelt down, opened it and shook his head in wonderment. 'We sure as hell hit the big one today, Wesley.'

'You going to take it all?' Murchison asked, his

Ride a Long Shadow

voice little more than a whisper.

The question surprised me and I guess it took Tobin wrong-footed as well. He turned back to the man in black. 'Why, you think we shouldn't, Rafe, you think we should give out equal shares to you and the boys here? You dumb asshole, of course I'm going to take it all.'

I wondered what had happened to the *we*, and, as I was wondering that, Murchison fired from between his legs, the bullet tearing into the pannier by Tobin's stooped-over figure.

A hideaway.

As the shot ripped out, Murchison rolled for cover and Luke Coy grabbed for his fallen pistol. Matt Coy was moving too as was the man called Leroy, but Luke had his pistol out of the leather and it was coming up. Off to my right, Tobin fired, twice, the rounds bouncing out of the dust at the disappearing Murchison. I shifted the shotgun on to Luke and pulled both triggers as I began my own move out of the line of crossfire between Murchison and Tobin. Even as I moved, I snapped open the shotgun, ejected the hulls and watched as Luke smashed back against the oak tree, his chest ripped open by the heavy buckshot. He hit the tree and stayed there, upright, head and arms hanging loose, dead as a hat, but not falling down. I wondered at that as I shoved in fresh loads and rolled for the shelter of the mine entrance, ending

Ride a Long Shadow

up looking out at nothing with the hot barrels of the Greener resting on the ribcage wherein once beat the heart of a long dead Comanche.

It was a mess. Worse than that, it was what I had feared most, a stand-off. Murchison, Matt Coy and Leroy out in the rocks and trees, Tobin and me in the mine and the clearing. As if reading my thoughts, Tobin called cheerfully, 'Don't sweat it, Wes, least we got the gold and they got squat.' He laughed and his laughter was greeted with a blast of gunfire from the trees. His rapidly returned fire brought a yell of pain and I peppered the area with buckshot causing more pain and panic. A man stood up and made for better cover: Leroy. Tobin shot him twice in the back and then switched his point of aim from the falling man to where two shots cracked back him. Reloaded, I blasted the area again. Then nothing, silence, the ringing in my ears and the stink of burnt powder in my nose and, much later, the fluttering of the doves as they returned to their roost in the rocks above.

It was a long day. The sun shifted the shadows across the narrow canyon and they lengthened and deepened purple into the late afternoon. I had no idea if Tobin was still where I thought him to be although I had a good idea that Murchison and Coy were as pinned down as was I.

Ride a Long Shadow

I was wondering about trying to improve my position when Murchison called out from behind his rock.

'Hey, Posy, you still out there?'

I waited but there was no reply, not that I really expected one.

'Posy, what say you and your partner take three panniers and go clear, leave me and Coy one each, that way we all get rich. Sure as Hell is hot, this way some of us won't make it out of here.'

'Where did you keep that hideaway hid, Rafe, up your ass?' Tobin called back to him then.

'Goddamn you, Posy, we go way back.'

Tobin didn't answer again and the afternoon dragged on and I began to fret about Fort Bowie, my conscience telling me I should have given up the gold and run for the fort. 'Give them half of it, Posy, we got enough and I got to get out of here, remember?' I called the words across to Tobin, but it was Murchison who answered.

'Listen to him, man, there's gold enough for all.'

'There's never enough, Rafe.' And this time the words came from Tobin and they came from the higher ground behind me, and Murchison understood. He broke for new cover to be brought down by two quick rounds from Tobin's Colt. He staggered and fell dust popping from the back of his black vest, tried to get up and went down cursing under a third and fourth round. Coy ran forward yelling and firing as he ran and I dropped him with the Greener, blew the side of his head away, the blood of both brothers now on my hands to join the night-time, nightmare ranks of the lonely dead I had killed in war, in the line of duty or, in this case, out of pure greed.

I stood up and Tobin scrambled down beside me; he was smiling. We moved forward to where Rafe Murchison was still trying to get to his feet. He stared up at Tobin who cocked his piece and casually shot the outlaw between the eyes, snapping the man's head back and stilling him forever.

I walked past the dead men to where Luke Coy still stood sentinel, propped up against the oak tree. I could not make out why he didn't fall and walked to the side of the body and suddenly understood. The legend had been correct in every detail; Luke Coy's back was punctured by the rusting head of a large pickaxe pike, the other end of the blade jammed deeply through the swollen bark and into the meat of the tree. Bowie's mark, fifty long years in the making.

We stripped the dead of their weapons and any papers that should be sent to their next of kin and dragged the bodies into the mine entrance, working together by the last fading rays of the sun. We set them down to lie side by side with the Comanche that Murchison claimed were victims

Ride a Long Shadow

of Jim Bowie all those long years before. True or false, it made little difference to any of them now. They were dead and only Bowie would be remembered, remembered and revered for his last defiant hours at the Mission San Antonio de Valero, better known as the Alamo, and not for the deaths of Comanche warriors whose gold he had very likely stolen. Once the dead were settled, we left and, dislodging a rotten pit prop, we toppled rock and rubble down around the entrance to entomb the men and to keep the coyotes away from their bodies. Tobin was silent while we worked, his mind on some place else far away from that bloody canyon. We rounded up the mules and loaded the five heavy panniers on their backs and, carrying the smaller bag and anything else we had salvaged, we made our way back out of the canyon.

The dead scarecrow of a man with the savage knife wound in his back was still propped up on guard. We had forgotten him in our haste to be clear of the area before nightfall. I reached for a shovel from one of the packs, but Tobin cursed and, stepping forward, he toppled the body over the edge of the slope and watched it roll before it jammed hard and fast into a narrow cleft. He kicked some loose rocks down on top of it and moved on to the canyon's narrow entrance back to where we had left the bay and Tobin's sorrel. The small bag was tied off behind my saddle and without a word or a single backward glance, we headed south for Maria, the cave and Fort Bowie. Only it didn't quite turn out like that.

EIGHT

Maria was delighted to see us, ignoring Tobin, but fussing over me as though I were her long lost father or, as it later became apparent, her long lost lover. She prepared a meal and fresh coffee for us from the provisions we had brought back from the mine and while we ate she rubbed down the bay, hobbled the mules and the burro just beyond our shelter – there now being too many animals to share the cave with us. From time to time, she cast a curious eye at the six heavy leather bags Tobin and I had hauled into the cave.

I wiped my plate and checked the pocket watch I always carried, it was a little after nine o'clock. the air was cool and sweetly scented with the odour of burning pine resin and the damp night-time smells that drift up from any fresh running water-course. An owl worked the fringes of the wood and called from his high perch. The call answered by a like minded bird, he flew on and once we heard his wings beating the air close by and, moments later, the death squeal of small rodent. Tobin took one of the small cigars he had taken from Murchison's bloody shirt-front pocket and offered me one. I'm not a real smoker, but I enjoy one now and again, although more than that, it was an opening, an opportunity to break the long silence that had occupied the distance between us since the vicious gunfight of the afternoon.

I struck a blue-top match with my thumb and fired the cigars. He drew deeply on the smoke and stared at me over the flickering match, a strangeness about his eyes, a shifting of focus. He pulled away and set his back against one of the panniers almost as though he were waiting for something to happen, for me to speak perhaps. I obliged him, there were things that had to be said, some could wait but one could not, other people's lives, soldiers, strangers mostly, depended on it.

'I'll be heading for Bowie come first light. Ride with me if you care to, Posy, if not then we'll split our share of the gold here and you can be on your way to Mexico with the Renaldos' cut. It's up to you really, whatever you think is fair and against whatever deal you made with the Renaldo family. I'll take the girl with me though, she can ride one of the spare horses.'

He did not answer right away, carefully exam-

Ride a Long Shadow

ining the lit end of his cigar like he might find in its glow a reply that would fit my unasked question.

'I don't think there will be a share for our south-of-the-border friends, Wes, we risked our lives for the gold; the best they did was gamble a little money, plenty of which they already have. No, this is between you and me.' He did not look at me, the cigar end seemed to hold some overriding fascination for him or, perhaps, it was merely a distraction.

I thought about what he had said for a minute or two. It was his decision, he had made the deal, whatever it was, with the Renaldos. It was not up to me to judge him for welching on that or for anything else he might have done. On the bright side, I felt a twinge of larceny myself. He was right, I had risked my life for the gold and a bigger share would not come amiss, but it was his deal. At the beginning, talking together by the dried-out White Hat Creek, back when I had agreed to ride with him, no mention had been made of an actual percentage. I had always assumed, reasonably I believed, that the danger equally shared meant an equal share of the reward with perhaps a slightly higher percentage going to him on account of him putting the play together in the first place.

I said, 'That's really up to you, Posy. I would

have been happy with whatever share of the finder's fee you had agreed with them, and still would be. However, if there is more. . . .'

'No more for you, Wes, I'm afraid I need the whole roll. Oh, of course, I'll give you a handful of gold to help you keep that two-by-four outfit of yours afloat, but that's as far as I'll go.' His voice was calm, his attention still on the stogie.

I stared across the fire at him. 'Come again?'

'You heard me right first time out, Wes, but I will make it clearer for you if you want me to. What I'll do is leave you one of the spare horses and a gold bar or two for wages, that's only fair, but the rest comes with me, I have plans for it, big plans.'

'Plans?' I tried to keep the anger out of my voice. 'Plans? What could you possibly need so much money for, it's more than you ever dreamed about already?'

'Dreams? What could you possibly know of my dreams, Wes? You're a sanctimonious son of a bitch out to set the world to rights, but not too worried if you make a dollar on the side while you're about it. Me, I'm a sure enough dreamer and a few dollars from a reward poster now and then for bringing in some poor stiff head down over a saddle won't cut it for me. I need more, much more.'

'What could you buy with all of it that you

couldn't buy with a fraction of it?'

He climbed to his feet and smiled that tired, red-eyed smile down at me. 'Texas, Wes, I'm going to buy the whole damn state if I can, politically that is.'

I started to get to my feet, unable to hold back the anger I felt at his dismissal of me; my way of life, my efforts in the recovery of the gold, the fort and its attack forgotten.

'Don't make me kill you, Harper.'

He had a pistol on me, the Colt drawn from a fold in the lap of his duster. It must have been there all through the meal, Tobin waiting for the moment to throw down on me, kill me in my sleep maybe.

'You got the guts to do that, Posy, shoot down a friend in cold blood?'

'They say that in politics there is no such thing as friendship, this'll be my first lesson.'

Out of the corner of my eye, I watched as Maria returned from checking the stock. She froze at the sight of the pistol pointing at my heart and then came on in. She ignored Tobin, walked past him and stooped down to the fire, then came up fast and threw the coffee pot at him. As he reeled away from the scalding liquid, I leapt across the fire, wrapping my arms around his waist, throwing him down, jarring the weapon from his hand and the two of us rolling clear of the cave, one minute

Ride a Long Shadow

with me on top and the next, beneath him. We ended up side by side in the near darkness and both of us reached our feet at about the same moment. He was swinging before he was up and I took the blow under my ribs with a grunt and smashed down on his face with my right hand, driving my knee upwards at the same time. He turned sideways on and took both blows, hitting back with a looping haymaker that made my ear ring as I bounced two fast lefts off his rock-hard gut. We slugged it out for several seconds. I was beating him and he knew it, moving backwards and away from me his hands protecting his face. My toe stubbed on a rock and, as I staggered forward, my balance lost, he drove his knee into my chest, winding me. As I reeled, gasping for breath, something harder than a fist bounced off the side of my head and I fell away into the pitch darkness that has little or nothing at all to do with the midnight hour or the passing of the sun.

I will never know whether or not Posy Tobin would have killed me with that pistol if Maria hadn't hit him first with the hot coffee. Certainly, later, he would have had the chance to kill me when I was defenceless and unconscious on the floor of the cave, but for some reason or other he had chosen not to.

According to Maria, when I was awake enough

Ride a Long Shadow

to understand her excited babbling, he kicked me once and then walked away from me, and, long before the morning, he was gone, as was the gold, the mules, burro, spare mounts and most of the provisions. He left me the bay, my gunbelt and revolver, my carbine and the Sharps. He also left me a single bar of gold and the woman, Maria. She cleaned my bloody face and the wound caused by the blow from Tobin's pistol barrel. He had, apparently, scooped that up from the ground while I knelt, winded and gasping, from the blow dealt me by his knee. Later she helped me walk around the clearing, supporting me for a while, helping to free my head of the pain and despair that filled me. Despair, not for the loss of the gold, but for the passing of time. It was after first light and still I had made no move to alert the garrison at Fort Bowie to the imminent danger from the Apache war party.

I drank down two cups of coffee and, halfway recovered, I quickly packed our gear together; then, with Maria riding behind me, her strong arms around my waist, I headed the bay down the hilly slopes to where the war party were camped when I had last seen them. I needed to check their progress before running blindly for the fort. The bay was fresh and we covered the downhill ground rapidly, passing the place where the lightning had blasted the tree and the rock where I

Ride a Long Shadow

had sheltered on the day of the storm. By midmorning, we were on the hillside above the Apache encampment and it was deserted. They had ridden west and I could still see the dust of their passing. We had missed them by minutes. I turned the bay after them and, keeping to the higher ground, although careful to keep clear of the ridges and staying above the tree-line where possible, rode him easily to a point near to the valley's mouth. In an hour, we were ahead of them, maybe only twenty minutes or so, but ahead nevertheless. I eased the bay to a stop and, sliding from his back, lifted Maria down and stripped the animal of everything other than saddle and harness, stowing the gear out of sight in a nearby thicket. Next I scribbled a pencilled message to Tom Alexander and gave it to her. She tucked the paper into her shirt pocket and looked at me expectantly. Waiting, wondering what I wanted next of her.

I rested both of my hands on her narrow shoulders and spoke slowly and clearly to her. 'Maria, you must go on alone now, ride to Fort Bowie, it's maybe fifteen miles to the west of here, a clear trail this high up. Give that note to the commanding officer, his name is Colonel Alexander. He is a friend of mine and he will know what to do and he will take care of you until I return. If you should run into a patrol of soldiers from the fort then give it the officer in command. It is a very important piece of paper. Do you understand all of that?'

She nodded. 'And what of the Apache? And what of you?'

'I'm setting myself up in those rocks above the trail. I'll slow them down, give Choya something to think about and then I'll head on back for the trees and get to the fort by foot, we'll pick up the gear later.'

'Choya?'

'He is a war chief; he leads the Apache.'

'You will be killed.'

'No, no, I won't, Maria, I will be very careful. Now you must ride. The bay is fresh and strong and with a light rider like you on his back he will fly. Be good to him; his name is Calico and, although I never use it, you can, he likes to hear it.'

The bay's ears pricked forward at the sound of the name and he turned his head towards me. I ran my fingers lightly over the soft muzzle and then the girl was in my arms, clinging to me, her bruised lips on mine, whispering in Spanish, soft words that had no meaning to me. I returned her kiss and then gently pulled away and helped her up on to the bay. I shortened the stirrup leathers and rocked the saddle under her, it was firm.

'You will be killed, Harper, I know this.' She said the words quietly, her eyes flooding with tears.

Ride a Long Shadow

'Don't bet on it, Maria, I'll see you again, you can count on that. Maybe I am, what would you say, *hombre viejo*, an old man? Well, let me tell you, young lady, I still got some living to do.' I winked at her. '*Vaya con Dios, Maria,* vaya con Dios' Then I gently slapped the bay's rump and watched the pair of them head out across the high ground and into the trees beyond. She did not look back and I was glad of that.

NINE

I climbed up on to the large flat rock that overlooked part of the valley through which the Apache rode. I was further ahead of them than I had thought. They were riding in a ragged, loose-knit line, headed for the mouth of the valley and the distant Fort Bowie. I had absolutely no doubt as to their intention or their destination. Maria had been gone for well over an hour, enough of a head start, I reasoned, should Choya feel it necessary to have a rider scout the open trail ahead of him. It was time. Like I had told the woman, I reckoned on slowing them down, giving them a bloody nose, something to think about, before I headed on out the back door and into the hills to make my own way back to Bowie on foot. Hit and run, a tactic that should prove familiar to them.

It would be a long walk.

Crouching on one knee, I set out a handful of the long bottlenecked, brass-cased .50 calibre rounds within easy reach of my right hand and settled myself down to load the big Sharps I had taken from the dead guard, the one Tobin had knifed back in Bowie's canyon. I dropped the block and slid a bullet into the breech, closed it again and with my elbow steadied by my raised knee, sighted on the nearest Apache. I judged the range to be around 500 or so yards. I set the double triggers, let my breath out slowly and capped the round. There seemed to be the briefest of delays following the kick in my shoulder before the man jerked backwards, somersaulting off the animal's back. There was a sudden confusion as riders milled their frightened ponies, looking to the left and the right of them, yelling and waving their weapons in the air. I reloaded the big rifle and fired again, missing the rider I was aiming for but dropping his horse right out from under him. He quickly leaped to his feet and up behind the nearest rider. I fired at that rider and both men toppled sideways and a pony at their rear stumbled and fell. The heavy round must have passed through both men with enough velocity still left in it to drop the animal as well. Its scarfaced rider ran for cover. I hit one more Apache on the run before the band dispersed and were lost to my view, hidden by the overhang of the rocky ledge I had chosen as my firing point. After a minute or two one man, less cautious than his fellows,

Ride a Long Shadow

popped his head up not 200 yards away from me and I blew it off. That was the last I saw of them for twenty minutes, so I decided it was time to run for the higher ground and be gone from that place.

That didn't happen.

Two rounds whined off the rocks to both my right and left, one of them scuttling my canteen over the rim. A third bullet buzzed over my head so close that I felt the whisper of its passing. They had quickly closed the back door and it looked like the side doors on me as well. I cursed and moved to the centre of the flat rock aware that just so long as I kept my head low they would not be able to get in a clear shot, that is unless they came a whole lot closer, and if they did that, I would be in as good a position as any to hold them off. I could not get back down to my carbine and pack though, which meant I only had the army issue Colt and my own sidearm. The Sharps was useless to me so I stripped out the block and tossed it into the gully before jamming a lead round in the barrel's mouth and tossing the rifle itself in the other direction. In case this was to be the Shadow Rider's last stand, I buried Grant's silver Colt in the deep sandy gravel of a rocky crevice just within reach of my left hand.

And that's the way it stayed for the rest of the early and late afternoon, the waiting Coyotero below, the hot sun above and me spread-eagled on the top of nowhere. The sun beat down on me the long hours and I yearned for water. My duster and hat offered me some protection, but my only real salvation was the breeze; scented with pine and sagebrush, it whipped over the higher ground, cooling me and drying me out at the same time.

I thought of home, wherever that was, of my wife Theresa who had counselled against my expedition with Posy Tobin. My life was full of questions, most of them unanswerable. Had Theresa been right, had my soul brushed against that of the Devil? Was Tobin the man I once knew and where had the fire in his eyes come from – within or without? And Jonah, the boy who worshipped me, saw in me something I could never see in myself, a strength he took for granted but was fading in me at that dark moment, what manner of man would he become? Old Moke would watch the night for me and weep like the others when my death was finally reported and yet he would never truly believe it. I thought of the cattle on my property running fat now I guessed, with water aplenty running from the windmills and the tanks all filled. And what of White Hat Creek? Had it rained? Was water again dancing beneath the willow trees? Then I thought of Maria and hoped she had made it safely to the fort and that Tom Alexander was ready for the brutal onslaught that would follow my demise

Ride a Long Shadow

which would, I supposed, come somewhere in the early evening when the Apache could attack with ease under the cover of darkness. I smiled at that thought. What dime novelist had written that Indians don't attack at night? Bullshit; they kill when it suits them and in any fight it suits them, day or night. Still, life had been good to me and I had six rounds in the Colt, five for the first wave and one for myself. Unlike life with its tangled and confusing ways, death was that simple.

And so I waited, sweated, daydreamed and, occasionally, I thought of Posy Tobin and our gold that he was running south, slowly, cautiously. And into my day-befuddled dreams there crept a plaintive sound, a distant wail that was not of the breeze's making.

A distant call on the wind, a brassy sound hidden from me by the flat-topped hill to my right. Then I heard it again, a whisper on the uplifted air, growing in volume by the moment. With great care not to expose my head above the rock's rim, I crawled to my right and, after removing my hat, I peered out across the empty valley's mouth – only it wasn't an empty valley anymore.

By its very nature, war is the creator of such powerful imagery that long after the moment, whether preserved by photograph or burnt into the mind of the beholder, it returns to haunt and remind a man of his absolute mortality. The stone wall at Chancellorsville, the canister-blasted trees of Wilderness, the dead of Gettysburg or the hallowed ground of Arlington Cemetery, each in its way serves to remind the observer of the horror of military conflict. And yet there are also stunningly beautiful and moving moments in war, fragments of a delicious glory that is best preserved in the mind's eye, for it is in the mind's eye alone that a moving picture can be retained and treasured for those desolate moments when war, any war, whatever the cause, is considered to be the only answer to man's infinite problems. Few such spectacles of battle can possibly match the full charge of expertly mounted riders as they plunge forward through the dust of the ages, to death or glory, their lathered horses striding, and their hearts beating time to a bugle boy they cannot see. Such a glorious sight met my tired, red-rimmed eyes as I cautiously peered around the edge of my rocky shelter.

A red sky at their back, an hour from sunset, sixty men riding line abreast, their chestnut horses at the high canter, riding out of a dust storm of their own making. In the centre and a mount's-neck length ahead of the line, Colonel Thomas Alexander, stiff-backed, his sabre at the present, the brim of his hat curled up into the wind. To his left and a little behind, his corporal

Ride a Long Shadow

orderly leading a riderless mount, its stirrup leathers flapping to the stride and, beside him, the company bugler. Each side of the leading three men, the colours, the American flag to the right and the blue and gold swallow-tailed guidon of the 6th Cavalry to the left. Even as I watched them coming on, Alexander's sabre suddenly pointed forward and flashed red in the late sunlight as he gave spur to his horse and leaned into the full charge. How they galloped, those long-striding horses, the time picked up by the bugler who missed a note then raised the call high above the thundering hooves.

It was a moment.

With a crazy disregard for my own safety, I leapt to my feet on the high rock that had protected me for the better part of the long day. I raised my arms aloft and cheered them forward at the top of my broken voice, my dry throat cracked as I barked my enthusiastic roar of approval at their being. Several rounds bounced off the rock at my feet and screamed away, but they did not still my voice, weaken my spirit nor shift me from my place of triumph. It was a madness that to this day makes me tremble and swallow hard at the lump raised in my throat by its memory.

The Apache broke and scattered for their panic-stricken, wide-eyed ponies. No more bullets came my way and the charging line broke into the running Indians. The sun lancing off flashing blades and puffs of gunsmoke and the popping of sidearms were part of the afternoon. The rider leading the loose mount broke from the line and headed to my roost at a parade-ground trot, seemingly oblivious to the turmoil around him. He reined in his own heaving mount at the base of the rock and turned the empty saddle towards me, saluting and yelling at the top of his excited young voice, 'Colonel Alexander's compliments, sir, he is pleased to offer you a ready remount from the US 6th.'

'My thanks to your colonel, son,' I shouted back. 'I accept his generosity with pleasure and gratitude.'

He grinned a toothy grin at me as I leapt aboard the unaccustomed small McClellan saddle, slipped my boots into the long stirrups, grabbed at the reins with one hand and, with my reloaded Colt in the other, I galloped after him and into the thick of the dusty battlefield.

It was over before ever we reached it.

The broken line turned to the bugle's recall and reformed on its commanding officer, forming a circle around the still billowing colours. I joined him in the centre there, fought my excited animal to a standstill and side-walked him to the side of Alexander's foam-flecked horse.

'Good to see you, Wes. Been a great morning,

the Old Man would have loved every moment of it.' His voice was a shout above the jangle of harness and the snorting of the horses. The grin was wide, his lips tight around a well-chewed, unlit cigar butt. He stuck out his free hand and I grabbed at it.

'Didn't expect to see you this afternoon, Colonel, or any afternoon come to that.'

'Got your message, didn't see the point of waiting for them to come for us. We were too few in number to defend both Bowie and the settlement. Brought with me every fit trooper who can sit a horse, even the goddamned company cook is in there somewhere.' He turned and bellowed, 'Where you at, Cooky, you still got your hair?'

'Yo, sir, safe and sound,' came a cheerful response from a fat, red-faced trooper with both of his meaty hands full of excited horse.

Alexander turned back to me, his voice lower. 'You don't hold too much with what we do out here, Wes, and I can't blame you for that, but I'd bet my last dollar we were a hell of a sight coming across that valley floor at the gallop.'

'One hell of a sight, Colonel, one I'll sure as hell never forget.'

And the tears welled into my eyes and he turned from me, I suspect, lest I saw the dampness in his own.

Ride a Long Shadow

*

We walked the horses back through the late evening darkness, raising again the settling dust of their earlier passing. The animals were spent as were the riders, and yet in memory of the fallen 7th, they sang; 'Garrywen' as they rode and then glanced at each other from time to time, glad they were alive, and that their charge had been triumphant. And a success it had most certainly been for not a soldier had fallen or been blooded by the startled enemy.

As battles went, it had not been a murderous one. Apart from several dead ponies and the five Apache I had killed earlier with the Sharps, there were only nine other corpses left to litter the valley floor, the remainder of the band had faded mysteriously into the landscape, drifted into the foothills and the trees, scattered like leaves before the wind of the 6th Cavalry. And Alexander was happy to let them go. Choya was not among the dead. He, like the rest, would head on foot or stolen horseback for the border. They would no doubt regroup and raid north again, but only in small bands, the real Apache way. The mighty hundred warriors he had somehow gathered together, were dispersed and would remain so, fiercely independent, a way of ilfe and battle confirmed for the better by the loss of the day.

Ride a Long Shadow

Alexander informed me that Maria and the bay were both exhausted but well and that the United States Army owed her a debt of gratitude that would be difficult to ever repay. Then, later, while the crippled Indian ponies were dispatched with pistol balls and the frightened strays rounded up and strung together head to tail for their journey back to Fort Bowie, the men bivouacked for coffee and the cleaning of arms. I took that moment to clamber back to my eyrie and dig up my Colt. I also retrieved my carbine, but I could not find the Sharps and was, in a way, glad of that. The rest of my trappings, including the gold bar, I would collect later when I rode that way again.

I slept in the saddle for most of the journey back to Fort Bowie, tired and weary beyond description. The exhilaration of the afternoon and early evening had quickly passed and my sleeping thoughts were with Posy Tobin and the long trail I had yet to follow.

TEN

'What happened to your partner, he run off with Bowie's gold?' Alexander laughed at his own answer to a question I had been waiting to hear all evening. We were sitting in his comfortable bachelor quarters drinking a celebratory after-supper brandy and smoking long cigars. The pot-bellied stove glowed red and the room was filled with a heady mixture of tobacco smoke, the tang of hard liquor and the lingering odour of the stew Maria had insisted on preparing for us. She had served it, watched us devour it and then, to Alexander's amusement, she had kissed me on the top of my head and left for the room allocated to her in the small row of officers' quarters, one of which was mine.

I had slept for most of the day following our weary but triumphant return to Fort Bowie, the dusty column greeted by cheers from the settlement dwellers and with quiet relief from the skeleton garrison of wounded men and army wives left behind to defend the fort should Alexander's plan fail. Bathed, shaved and in clean clothes bought at the sutler's, I looked almost human behind the purple bruises left over from my fist fight with Tobin less than forty-eight hours before.

'I guess you could say that, Tom, he got most of it anyway.'

My unexpected reply silenced him and the smile faded. He ran his hand through his long grey hair, twitched at his moustache and looked generally uncomfortable. I teased him, waiting for him to break the silence and topping up my glass conscious of the dangerous feeling of warmth and well-being drifting over me.

'Hey, Wes Harper, you really found it, didn't you. Goddamn, I would never have believed it possible, you couldn't have ridden more than thirty miles from here.'

'Twenty about, it was in an old box canyon you couldn't see for rock falls. We didn't have a map ourselves, but we knew a man who did have one and we followed him, followed *them* actually. They found the mine and we killed them in a better than fair gunfight which I will report in full at the Ranger station in Uvaldi and to the local law hereabouts if they want to hear it.'

Alexander leaned towards me, curiosity and

Ride a Long Shadow

interest in his set expression. 'I guess I'm what you call the law hereabouts, Wes, and I sure would like to hear the truth of it.'

I told him the whole story then, about the drought and my near ruin, and ex-Texas Ranger Posy Tobin riding out of the heat with a fantastic offer of unbelievable wealth that I had found hard to refuse and, in the end, impossible to turn down. I went right back to the beginning of it. To the map and the wounded Mexican soldier at the Alamo, and on to the old Apache, the killings in Newell County and the inevitable gunfight in the Hill Country with Rafe Murchison and his gang. And, finally, I told him of Tobin's duplicity and how the next morning I was going to saddle the bay, provision up and ride after him. I told my friend coldly in the flickering of the oil lamp, how I was going to give Tobin just one chance to give it up and knowing he would not take that chance, how I was going to kill him, gun him down like the double-crossing son of a bitch he really was.

'I don't believe we found the main shaft though, there were very few workings there, maybe it was a vent or an exploratory tunnel. It was a silver mine by the way, the gold we found was old, Spanish, a cache I guess. Ol' Bowie must have found that elsewhere and stored it with the silver he very likely stole from the Comanche. A lot of money moving south and half of it is mine, I

Ride a Long Shadow

guess, if Tobin's backhauling on the Renaldo family.'

'Is it worth it, I mean even so much money as that, is it worth risking your life twice for? Why not cut your losses and go with the bar you have hidden away, pay off your debts and raise your boy.' He was a softly spoken man and his words had a ring of sincerity to them.

'It isn't the gold, Tom. That might have been part of it back there in the cave when we were going at it, but it isn't that now. It's the fact that he left me and the woman alone, not knowing whether or not I would recover in time to warn you about Choya. He sold his soul to the Devil for Bowie's gold and damned near sold mine along with it, and for that I am going to bring him down, gold or no gold.'

Alexander leaned back in his chair, away from me, keeping his distance and I was miserably aware of how the words had come out. I guess I had sounded little better than the men I used to ride down. I relaxed. 'Sorry, Tom, didn't mean it to come out like that. You know. . . .' I left it there.

'That's OK, in a way I do understand the meaning of it and know that this garrison's very existence is probably due to you. The thing is though, you made it, you and the girl saved our hides and we are thankful for that. You are free of whatever devil haunted you back then, why conjure it up

Ride a Long Shadow

again? It's done, leave it lay and praise God you made it through the night. There I go, sounding off like a preacher man.' He laughed at himself, and changed the subject. 'What are you going to do about Maria, take her with you?'

I nodded. 'I promised her I would get her back to her village before going home; she works in the Mission Hospital there I believe, and I owe her that.'

We stood up and I reached out and shook his hand.

'Goodnight, Wes, whatever you do is all right with me and the US Army, I guess. Just take care is all. I'll be up to see you both off in the morning. Hell, what a letter I'll have to write the Old Man.'

I closed the door behind me and stretched my arms wide and rolled my neck on my shoulders trying to ease the irritation I felt, the anger at myself for speaking words that would inevitably burden my new friend. The cigar bounced where I flicked it on to the hard parade ground sending a little shower of sparks into the black night, I stepped down from the wooden porch and ground it out. A sentry called and was answered. Walking back to my room I was touched by the smell of the evening. Roses? Yes, roses. I remembered then Alexander telling me how one of the sergeant's wives was growing roses out back of the stable, close to a ready pile of fertilizer. The perfumed

Ride a Long Shadow

fragrance mixed in pleasantly with the earthier scent of the western night, crushed sagebrush, burning pine logs, horses and oiled tack. I smiled, heady from the brandy, not unsteady on my feet but a little disorientated in my thinking. I opened the door of my quarters and, without turning up the oil lamp, I slumped on to the edge of the bed, struggled out of my boots, pants and shirt and rolled right back on to it, startled by the softness of the woman. Her whispered words and soft hands reached out to me, touching me. I have no excuse for what followed, not even a reason other than the fact that maybe, that night of all nights, we needed each other and, conveniently, we were there for one another. I spoke her name only once. I whispered it 'Maria,' and then her lips were against mine and I tasted the sweetness of her mouth and later her soft, young, yet wholly womanly body.

The US Army gave me a mount for Maria, a soft-mouthed chestnut, too small for a cavalry horse but strong of wind and pleasant of disposition. Alexander was as good as his promise and was at the gate to see us off at first light whilst all but the sentries still slept, offering no parting words of wisdom other than to warn me of a still volatile situation with the Apache and to keep to the high ground. I promised to write and, with Maria at my

Ride a Long Shadow

side and a pack horse behind us, we set off for the hill where I had hidden the gold and the rest of our trappings.

Everything was as we had left it and I stowed our gear on to the pack animal anxious to be away from the battleground of two days ago. There was little sign that a battle, albeit a minor one, had taken place there and that armed men had tried desperately and, as it happened, quite ineffectually, to kill, wipe each other out. The dead ponies had been pretty well stripped by coyotes and buzzards leaving lean picking for the crows and the jays that hopped over and through the naked rib cages and skull bones. The dead, Alexander had insisted on leaving where they had fallen and he was right and wise to do that. The Apache must have returned soon after our departure and made off with their own comrades, to be disposed of in their own mystical ways. The only sign that remained of my own stand on the high rock was a small scattered pile of .50 calibre cartridge cases. They would stay there to corrode or to be found by some wanderer and pocketed as souvenirs of the Apache wars, perhaps the last remnant of a great and imagined battle to be talked about and drunk over at some saloon bar or around a distant campfire.

We quickly passed on by, heading for Tobin's cold trail.

Ride a Long Shadow

We rode hard until an hour before sunset where we crossed a clear running stream and I found a rocky overhang we could use as a shelter. The small fire I lit cooked our supper and boiled the coffee. After the pots and pans were cleaned and stowed away, we sat by the fire and Maria moved up close to me, shared my blanket and placed her raven-haired head gently upon my chest. I stroked her forehead and wondered what to tell her, how to tell her that there could be nothing more between us other than respect and an undying friendship. I owed her my life and I owed her for a very special shared night of passion. They were debts I could no longer repay in the way she needed, wanted.

'It's all right, Harper, you don't have to say nothing, I know you got a woman you love very much down along the Neuces, the soldier colonel told me this.' Her voice was soft, sleepy, almost smoky. I started to move my fingers away but she reached up and held them there. 'She is one lucky woman, but you know what, Harper, I'm the lucky one at this moment, I have my head on your chest and you are holding me and it will be that way until I am back in San Miguel and then you will go home and we will never forget our days together. Is that good for you?'

'It's good for me, Maria, it's very good for me.' I said quietly, relieved in one way but feeling even

Ride a Long Shadow

more guilty in another.

And so we travelled through the next five days and nights, partners more or less, and slowly closing the gap between Tobin and ourselves with every step of the way. Several times we cut his trail and lost it again. Once a small Ranger patrol shared our campfire and told us of an unfriendly man and several pack horses having crossed their trail the previous day, barely ten miles from where we camped. I asked if they knew him and they told me no, he was a stranger to them and seemed to want to stay that way. They said he was heading for the Chisos Mountains. They had also seen Apache sign but nothing fresh enough to warrant closer attention. Young men, lean and keen, four of them, perhaps too new to the job to have known Possum Tobin, although I bet they had heard tell of him. I didn't ask though and in the morning we waved to them as they rode out.

If the Rangers had run across Tobin and he was heading for the Chisos Mountains then I guessed he would be heading for the border and Coahuila and from then on, for God alone knew where. If I was going to stop him, then it had to be on the Texas side of the line which meant a harder ride for the two of us. I told Maria this as we broke camp. She wasn't too happy about the Chisos and I understood why.

ELEVEN

Inhospitable to man for a good many reasons, the Chisos Mountains rise out of the desert floor like the Devil's shoulder. They run the border of the Big Bend and are wooded where water flows to the Rio Grande following the infrequent rainfalls. Cougar live and hunt its rocky ledges and wooded canyons and, higher up, the golden eagle and falcons ride the wind searching the high peaks for the the unwary mammals who themselves pursue the spiders and lizards of the lower plains. But it was more than that to the woman; even more frightening than the possibility of Choya walking its wild trails to her were the stories of the Chisos ghosts, the night lights that burned the midnight hour seen from afar and gone when you finally reached their point of origin. It was said that the Devil rode the Chisos and the *chindi*, the spirits of the dead, Navaho, Apache and white man, were at his beck and call. I sensed her fear, a genuine reluctance to follow me and smiled at her the condescending way that 'educated' whites have with the supposedly ignorant, itinerant peoples of the West. I had my Colt and Winchester, didn't I? What could out run a .45 calibre bullet? She was not convinced by my reassurance and I laughed at her as she pulled in closer to me, her eyes wide, her discomfort growing by the hour as we left the flat desert land and moved the animals upwards as fast as the terrain would allow to the higher rocky ground beyond the wild flowers and the cottonwoods that roamed the banks of a narrow creek.

Earlier that morning we had passed an old adobe building, its walls crumbling with time and neglect and within the confines of its three standing walls I had found fresh horse manure, the remains of a very recent campfire and two stogie butts. The telltale sign told me that less than twenty-four hours before we reached it, that old long-abandoned dwelling had given night shelter to three horses, two mules, a burro and one white man. Posy Tobin was less than a day ahead of us and I checked my weapons with great care before continuing on, even to the extent of placing a sixth round under the hammer of the Colt, something prudent gunfighters and lawmen rarely do.

We saw white tail and mule deer and once,

Ride a Long Shadow

around midday, I fancied I heard a distant rifle shot but could not be certain of it. In mountains where rock falls are constant, crumbling granite can crack and the sound, distorted on its journey downwards, can, like the call of the eagle or the bark of a deer, be identified as a dozen different things. Nevertheless, I slowed our progress and slipped the hammer thong from off my pistol.

That first night in the mountains we cold camped. If Tobin were close by he might see our fire or, more likely, smell the woodsmoke as it drifted up to the higher ground. Jerky, biscuits and cold water served us well enough and after settling the animals and making sure Maria was warmly tucked into her bedroll, I climbed up through the trees and out on to a rocky moonlit plateau. The moon was growing to half full and the clear air seemed to act as a conduit to its bright white light, magnifying it and lighting the countryside ahead of us. I could not see a fire or smell man. A mountain lion passed me by as I sat quietly on a fallen piñon. Seeing me suddenly, he whipped around and snarled at me, his teeth flashing yellow in the light, and then, with tail high, he ran the grass and disappeared among the shadowed rocks. The Devil? I imagined a Mexican hunter sitting on my piñon, a bellyfull of tequila or mescal, seeing the yellow face, the red eyes and hearing the hissing snarl as it passed him by. The yarn he would tell the following morning, the story of how old Nick himself waltzed by him, almost touched him and let him be. A warning perhaps. Then there was something else, a distant sound that entered my dreaming thoughts of Satan and drunken hunters, a voice or the wind through the high trees. I cocked my head and moved across the clearing. The sound faded and then came back, drifting down, broken by the evening breeze, disjointed for a moment and then clear. It was a man singing. Tobin, up there alone in the high country, needing the sound of another voice, scared of the Devil perhaps. Posy Tobin singing 'Amazing Grace' to the tired horses in a deep, tuneful baritone voice. The sound of it made me shiver and I quickly made my way back to the camp, pulling my blankets around me and snuggling up to the sleeping Maria for extra warmth and comfort.

In the morning I found his campsite. Several stogies littered the ashes of a cold fire, a fire I had not seen. Close by, the vegetation was flattened by the animals and, amongst the debris of the night, I found an empty whiskey bottle. From Murchison's pack I supposed and wondered if there were more. We closed the distance that day, by how far I wasn't sure but I did know we were moving faster with our lightly packed animals than he could weighed down as he was

Ride a Long Shadow

by Bowie's gold and silver. Strange how I still thought of it as belonging to Jim Bowie, like maybe we should never have found it and it should have stayed hidden, a chalice to be sought out for all time. The mountains were getting to me, the thin air or the mystery and the magic accepted by the native Apache and the wandering Mexicans but disavowed by men like Tobin and me.

Evening came with a rush that late afternoon as great black clouds seemed to gather out of nowhere above our heads, rolling clouds lit silently from within by flickering lights as the thunder tried to escape the confines of the high peaks and the granite of the Chisos. Struggling into our slickers, we found shelter just as the first great raindrops rattled on to the brim of my hat. Not quite a cave but close enough. A giant flat slab of grey, moss-covered rock had, centuries ago, slid down a sheer rock face, digging its edge into the shale at the cliff's base and there formed a huge lean-to, the one open side in the lee of a crumbling bank, the other partially sheltered by scrub and stunted pine. It was large enough for the animals and for us. I led them to the far side of the shelter and unsaddled them while Maria gathered dry wood for a fire I had reluctantly agreed she should light. The rain would keep the smoke down low and it was unlikely the flames would be seen from above. Apart from the mist of the splashing rain, the overhang protected the interior from view of anything short of an eagle.

I believe that we were both aware that we were close to the end of our long trail and, win, lose or draw, our days together were rapidly drawing to a close. After supper she stroked my hair and we made love together. Later, lying there in the near darkness, the fire flickering and the storm raging above our heads, I thought of Theresa and whether I should tell her of my infidelity or leave it to sleep there like the Comanche in Bowie's cave, for all time. It was something for me to think about. The storm passed, the thunder drifted off to the south and only occasional flickering of light told me the direction it was running: Mexico. The Bravo would be difficult to cross following the rain, I wondered if that thought had occurred to Tobin. Taking great care not to disturb Maria, I climbed out of my blanket, stretched and walked out of the shelter. The air was crisp and clean. I worked my thick jacket out of the pack, shrugged into it and, pulling up the fleece collar, I stepped out on to the shale-covered ground that shelved away from the rock face. The shaved moon was low over the highest peak, dodging the fast running clouds as they dispersed southwards. I fixed my gaze on the distant, shadowed heights wondering if Tobin had more liquor and wishing I had thought to buy some in the sutler's store at Fort Bowie. There was no singing tonight and even had there been, the breeze and the constant dripping of water would have kept it from my ears.

But it didn't and I heard it again. Closer, tuneless now like the man was really drunk, a baying almost, it drifted down to me and then stopped.

'What was that, Harper?'

I jumped at the sound of her voice as she joined me in the open, her voice still sleepy, her blanket wrapped around her shoulders keeping in the hard-earned warmth of our joined bodies and the dying fire.

'A bear,' I lied, putting my arm around her shoulders, feeling her hair on my unshaved cheek. 'A cougar maybe or even a javalina, they grunt and snort like a drunken man.'

'Javalina are not this high and neither do I believe it was a mountain lion.' There was a great fear in her whispered words and I tightened my arm around her.

'Up here it could have been one of a dozen things, animals, birds, hell, even the rocks make noises at night when the sun goes down and they crack with the cold. Who knows, this rain, the thunder, anything. . . .'

It came down to us again, only closer, clearer

and it wasn't singing, it was talking, shouting, and the words were directed at me.

'You come any higher, Harper, you dog my trail for another day and I'll kill you, you can count on it. And when you're dead I'll take the woman you dragged up here, and when I've had her hard I'll set her down beside you and leave you both there in the open, unburied and waiting for the animals.'

Automatically I pushed the woman behind me and drew my Colt, crouched over like I was in some dusty main street waiting for the play. The clouds tossed shadows across the open ground and even though the gun was useless to me, I held it, pointed its round muzzle towards the distant tree-line.

'Could have dropped you yesterday, Harper, but didn't; tomorrow, though, I will, you come any further.' There was a slight slurring to his words.

'The busthead getting to you, Posy, you met the Devil up here yet? You do, you buy him off with some that gold. Our gold, dead men's gold.' I couldn't keep the angry edge out of my voice and didn't try too hard to do so.

He laughed at me. 'Good old Harper, sleeping with a Mex whore and telling me I'm afraid of the Devil. Who do you see when you close your eyes at night, Wes, Jesus or old Nick?'

Ride a Long Shadow

I don't know why I did it, it was either madness or guilt; whichever it was it was done before I even thought about it. I fanned the hammer of the Colt sending six .45 slugs into the darkness aimed roughly at the sound of his cackling laughter. The reports racketed around the rocks and the arroyos, deafening me and sending Maria to her knees with her hands pressed hard to the side of her head. As the ringing in my ears faded, his laughter rose to a higher pitch and then stopped as suddenly as it had begun.

I waited, rodding out the empties and reloading from my jacket pocket.

'That's it, Harper, that's all you get. You come any higher and I'll kill you sure enough.' Then the singing again, softer, this time, 'Old Paint', the nighthawk's song, fading as he moved higher and then silence, either because he had stopped singing or because he had turned a corner and the sound could no longer carry down to me.

'Let us go back down, Harper. Take me home, go home yourself. He is the Devil and he will kill us both.'

'I'll be damned if I will,' I snarled at her without turning, a great coldness in me for all things, Tobin under my gun my only thought.

'Very probably, my love, very probably.' And then she too was gone, back into the comparative warmth of the cave and I was left standing there my loaded gun in my hand and nothing save shadows to shoot at.

TWELVE

It was a long, bad night for me, Tobin had disturbed me just as he had intended. Had I been on my own it would probably have been different, I might even have tried for him out there in the rain-soaked upland. As it was I slunk back into the shelter and wrapped myself in my blanket fighting the chill and the nightmare of sleep. I slept once and dreamed of the gunfight by the entrance to the mine. It was dark in my dream, midnight and our gun flashes lit up the clearing as lightning would do, flickering and white. Each bullet strike caused a fire and Murchison was blazing alight from head to toe as the rounds ripped into him. And when the fight was over it was total darkness and I could hear Tobin moaning. I fired a match to show him where I was and as the light flared, he blasted me with the shotgun. The muzzle flash lit up the mine and I could see that the entrance had caved in and we were all dead, stretched out side by side in the darkness with the skeletons of the two Comanche. And Tobin was laughing. I awoke with a start, terrified that I couldn't see anything, believing the dream to be real. I calmed down and the woman stirred beside me. My eyes became accustomed to the darkness and one of the horses snorted and I knew I was safe.

The night held other irritations for me and with the first light, when I tried to stand up, the pain in my right leg was such that I sat back down again. The cold and the damp had filtered through my chaps and Levis and the leg, always susceptible to bad weather, had given out on me. It ached and it hurt to move it. Maria told me to sit still while she boiled some water. I didn't argue, watching as she stoked up the fire, blowing on the embers filling the lean-to with the perfume of burning pine resin. It crackled and sparked as it burned. She brought me hot coffee and two large stones she had heated at the fire's edge, wrapped in an old shirt. She made me drop my pants and set the stones either side of my thigh. The pain eased almost immediately. She looked at the puckered entrance and exit scars, curious as to their origin.

'A man named Arkansas Bob Deacon, an outlaw killer, shot me through both thighs one time, near crippled me.'

Ride a Long Shadow

'And what happened to this man?'

'Couple of years ago, I caught up with him along the Arkansas River and killed him.[1] I was wearing a badge back then.' I added that to make it sound less dramatic, less cold; it made little difference, she moved away from me and sat on the pack staring at me.

'You have killed many men, Harper?'

'More than I care to remember.'

'You were dreaming of some of them last night when you called out?'

'Forget it, Maria. You've done a job on my leg; any more of that coffee in the pot, we need to be gone from here? Tobin knows we are following him and he will move quickly.'

'Or not at all.'

'What do you mean?'

'Now he knows you are here he may wait for you, shoot you from the trees like he promised last night.' She looked worried and I was sure it was concern for me and not out of worry for her own safety.

'No, he won't do that. He's warned us and now he will go on, pick his spot and make it happen. He knows I won't turn back.'

'Why not turn back, find another trail to Mexico. A safer trail.'

[1] See *Shadow on a Dark Mountain*.

'Can't do that.'

'Tell me why you cannot.'

'Maria, I don't believe I can do that either.'

I stamped some life back into my leg, watching her, amused at the pout exaggerated by her still swollen lower lip. Her eye was much better, still shaded purple, but open and glaring at me with its dark twin. I smiled, rubbed the back of my hand down her cheek and said, 'Thanks for fixing my leg, it's a whole lot better now than it was.'

'You are welcome, my lover,' she said simply, smiling and walking away from me, rolling her hips, over to where the steam was hissing from the spout of the chipped enamel coffee pot.

I was wrong about Tobin not bushwhacking us although I don't believe he actually intended to kill me, he was far too good a shot for that. He was only looking to scare me and he did that right enough. We had gone about a mile moving steadily upwards, the vegetation thinning out and giving way to less aggressive forestation. Short scrubby piñon, stunted oak trees and sagebrush littered the open areas, some good grass here and there but mostly shale and sharp, moss-covered rock. It was hot with the high sun beating down on us after the cold of the night. The rocks steamed away the rain and several times a golden eagle circled us, curious as to why man should be

Ride a Long Shadow

wandering that desolate place and disturbing his hunting.

We had, only moments before, cleared the treeline when something buzzed close by my ear. Even as I identified the sound as that of a passing bullet it was followed almost immediately by the confirming crack of a rifle. I swung my horse around, grabbed the chestnut's reins and galloped back to the shelter of the trees. Three more bullets sang past us followed by distant laughter drifting down from the rocks above. I cursed, jumping to the ground, jerking my carbine from the saddle boot and levering a round into its empty breech. But I had no target, no puff of smoke, or reflected sunlight to shoot at.

'I told you he would wait for us.' She was trembling.

'Then he will have to wait one hell of a long time because I know where he's going and there's lots of ways to get there first.'

I had a plan, I usually did have once I slowed down and stopped long enough to think things through. Tobin was headed for Mexico, he had to be, there was no other reason for his crossing the Chisos Mountains. He would feel safe in Mexico and for every dollar's worth the gold would buy north of the border it would buy double or even treble south of the Rio Bravo. He would fort up, make his deep plans and then come back and, what was his dream? Buy Texas? The man was either mad or he had a whole lot better understanding of politics than I did. I leaned against a tree thinking about it, the woman watching me waiting, hoping I supposed, that we would turn back. We would, but not right back. I had it figured that we could travel a whole lot faster with the one pack animal than Tobin could with his string of mules and the burro. He knew that, was why he wanted to slow us down, turn me around. I figured he had given me my last chance though, should he see me behind him again it would be goodnight Maria for sure.

'You have a plan, Harper?' she asked.

I turned to her. 'Everyone's always asking me if I got a plan, now why do you suppose that is?'

'You look like a man who makes plans.'

'Devious huh?' I added, with a reassuring smile. Maria shrugged her shoulders and fidgeted with the chestnut's bridle, looking away from me and up to where the shots had come from.

'He frightens me that man Tobin, he is. . . .' She struggled for the words. '*El Diablo*; he walks with the Devil, it is the *loco* fire of his eyes.'

My plan, if you could call it that, was a simple one. Ride back down the mountain, head either left or right, whichever way offered the better trail, and, by riding all night, gain a day on Tobin and come out somewhere below him and wait. He would know it was a course I might take and he would be wary, but there was little or nothing he could do about it. He could not, would not abandon the gold and at their best pace the pack train could only move at about a quarter of the speed we could travel if we really went for it. And I was going for it, driven by something I had no control over. It had become more than deserting the men at Fort Bowie, bigger than depriving me of my fair share of the gold. It was a passion, an obsession, not to kill the man, but to face him down fair and square, tell the son of a bitch what I thought of him and leave the rest to him. It was childlike in a way. No doubt Maria thought I was *loco* as well. Could be she was right; in all of my years behind a badge, never did I want anything so much as to stand in front of Possum Tobin and ride his play to the end.

THIRTEEN

We made the time I thought we would and cleared the fringes of the mountain well before first light. We had ridden fast by the moon then slower by starlight, stopping once for a cold meal and stream water, blowing the horses and moving quickly on. As the pale sun cleared the eastern horizon for what promised to be another hot day, we made camp among the live oaks and waited for Tobin to come down off his mountain. Mexico was less than three miles to the south of us.

He broke from the trees a little before sunset and unhurriedly led the pack animals over a rim and down into a rocky, high-walled canyon. Before cresting the ridge, he turned in the saddle and studied the high ground behind him through a pair of army field-glasses then, satisfied we were no longer behind him, he kneed his mount forward and over the edge, disappearing from our horizon.

Ride a Long Shadow

'Damned if we didn't do it, Maria,' I crowed, a little smugly I suppose, but it felt good to be right. We knew where he was and he had no idea at all where we were. His sights were firmly set on the border now and he would be over it by mid-morning and so lost among the steep hills, mountains and canyons of the rugged country that ran the banks of the Sabinas River, familiar country to him and the last resting place of the Apache, Ten Ponies, the man who had started it all for some of us and ended it for others.

We made our second cold camp in a row, our bedrolls spread out on the soft needle-covered ground on a pine-studded slope less than a mile from where Tobin was camped. I could not settle, wandering the night, nervous of the morning and scared the cold of the night would do my leg a mischief and rob me of any edge I might have over Tobin. I did have an edge though, I was the better shot. Not the faster draw, but the better man with a Colt. I knew that from our days together as lawmen, fighting the Kiowa and bringing in the *bandidos* and *pistoleros* who roamed the wide spaces of the South-West, a long time ago, back when we shared a common enemy.

'Why can't you sleep, you in too much of a hurry to kill this man?' Maria said, pulling her blanket away from her face and staring out into the darkness at me.

Ride a Long Shadow

'Checking the stock is all.' I offered lamely.

'You checked it twice already. Come here and I'll keep you warm, wrap my thighs around your sick leg.' She was teasing me and I was in no mood for it.

'Go to sleep, woman. You'll wake the dead.'

'Maybe they need waking, this madness is all about you. It is the Chisos, it is why they are here, to hold the spirits of the dead. Tomorrow, maybe it will be your spirit that walks here and I will cry for you.'

Leaving the pack horse tethered to a mesquite and with Maria beside me – she insisted on that and nothing I could say would dissuade her from it – I led the bay through the early morning light to the brush-covered ridge a little above the rim of Tobin's canyon. He was seated on a flat rock with his back to us, stirring the remnants of his night fire with a stick. There was a coffee pot sitting crookedly on the hot ashes and the smell drifted up to us making the saliva glands in my mouth tingle. We had slept cold while he had a fire, a hot supper and was beginning his day with a cooked breakfast. His horse and mules were gathered in a small brush corral which looked as if it had been there for a long time and used often. Rustlers, I wondered, a staging point between Texas and the markets in Chihuahua? Or Apache? I had no

Ride a Long Shadow

answer to my question and so dismissed it.

I slipped out of my canvas jacket and buttoned my vest all the way up. Next I checked my Colt, opened the loading gate and slipped in a sixth round. I spun the cylinder checking each chamber then, satisfied my silver killing machine was working to its maximum efficiency, I eased it back in to the oiled leather holster. It was snug against my belly, I drew it once and it came clear without a rub.

'Don't go.' There was a kind of desperation in her voice I did not like to hear, did not want to hear. 'Please, Harper, don't go.'

I ignored her request saying instead, 'If I don't make it back, take the bay at a run and head south for the border, you will be all right. Here' – I bent down and slipped the derringer out of my boot – 'take this, my Winchester is on the saddle and the gold bar in my saddle-bag. Ride like hell, I don't believe it is in him to hurt you, but with the gold around he's unpredictable. Take care, girl.'

I didn't wait for her to acknowledge my brief farewell, and instead turned to the rim of the canyon, walked up to it and over it. I made no secret of my approach and he half turned towards me before I had gone ten yards along the sage and rock-littered floor.

'Hi, Wes, wondered if you'd go low and around,

it's what I would have done was I you. Coffee? I guess you made a cold camp last night.' His tone was friendly enough and he did not seem at all surprised to see me. He waved his hand towards the coffee pot that sizzled away on the red coals, welcoming me like I was an old friend dropped by to chew the fat and maybe talk over old times.

'I don't believe I will, Posy, I came for the gold, or I came for you and to tell you the truth, I'm not sure which way around it is.' I laid the words on him in a whisper, my voice quite devoid of the emotion I felt at that moment, standing there on that timeless mountain ready to kill or be killed and for what? For the gold or because a sick man had broken his word to me?

Tobin climbed slowly to his feet and turned fully around to face me. He looked tired, his face even thinner than I remembered it. There were dark bulges beneath his eyes and his moustache drooped like wet grey moss over his narrow mouth. He was around seventy yards away, a longer than fair distance for handguns.

'Not much difference between the two reasons is there, Wes, either way you have to go through me.'

I walked towards him closing the distance to forty yards and stopped, set my legs and hooked the thumb of my left hand in my belt, my right hand I held towards my belly and six inches out.

Ride a Long Shadow

He cleared his jacket away from his tied-down revolver and with his other hand he pulled the brim of his hat low and toyed with the long ends of his grey moustache. Forty yards out and I could sense the anger in him, feel it, see the bright red of his eyes as he faced me down.

'Better get her done then, Wes, you're not touching my gold and that's for damned sure.' As he snapped out the words his hand dipped down and came up with the Colt.

Even as I pulled my own gun and fired straight-armed, I saw the flame leap at me and heard the round ricochet off the rock to my left. He fired again as did I, several times. The canyon was filled with the cracking reports of our weapons and the thin air thick with the burnt powdersmoke. I heard his bullets passing, felt one tug at my vest, another at my hat and then I saw him rock, take a shuffling backwards step with the impact of my round striking him, sending him away and down. He staggered back to his feet as my hammer fell on a spent casing and then he sighed and toppled forward and down. This time he stayed there.

'Jesus, Wes, you shot me dead.'

I walked slowly towards him, stopping beside the fire, smelling the hot coffee, bending towards him and wishing it were some other morning of some other day.

FOURTEEN

He was down, lying forward, his head towards me, propped up on one elbow, the gun still pointing in my direction. I straightened, dropping my gun hand to my side, the empty Colt pointing at the ground.

'How many you got left, Wes?' he asked, his voice weary.

I shook my head, but did not speak.

'I got just the one left myself, I'm not as quick as you,' he whispered.

'Give it up, Posy. Let me get you to a doctor, Fort Davis or below the border.'

'You'd do that, too, wouldn't you, you self-righteous son of a bitch?' He was smiling through blood-flecked lips, the moustache darkly stained. There was no anger in his voice, only sheer incredulity. 'You'd pump me full of lead and then tote me on your shoulders to a sawbones if you had to, get me well and send me home with a slap on the back.'

'It's what I do, partner.'

'Partner?' He coughed and smiled and the muzzle of the gun wavered. 'I guess we were partners there for a while, weren't we?' I took a half step forward and he brought the gun up on to my belly, snapped back the hammer. 'Partnership's dissolved now, so you'd best stay where you're at.'

'You need help and you know it, at least let Maria take a look at the wound.'

'Wound? Wounds you mean. You're a fair shot with that short-barrelled piece over a distance, Wes, put two in my brisket and one in my chest.' As if to confirm the latter he coughed dark blood on to the dust. He studied it for a moment, panic briefly dancing across his ashen face. 'Shit, I'm a goner for sure.' He looked up at me again and then across to where the panniers were heaped beside his smouldering fire. 'Move this way, pick up the small leather bag then step clear.'

'Why?'

'Do it man or I'll kill you where you stand.'

I jammed my piece back into its holster and, carefully stepping around him, picked up the leather bag. It was surprisingly heavy. I looked down at him. waiting.

'Now step back where you were.'

I did as I was told, then stood there holding the heavy bag.

'That'll do you, Wes, you and chicken-shit ranch of yours.'

'What do you have in here, Posy?'

He ignored the question. 'Clear the animals out of that Apache corral.'

I didn't move.

'Do it, damn you, man.'

I walked to the makeshift corral and dragged some of the brush away, walked in behind the startled animals and hit a couple of them across their rumps with my hat, I yelled some too, and they took off at a run, out and over the rim, kicking and running.

'The woman with you?'

'She's up on the ridge watching us.'

'Good.' He looked around and above him to where the rocky walls of the canyon leaned inwards, cutting out the sunlight, filling our lives with long shadows. He seemed satisfied and turned his attention back to me. 'Get going, get over that hill and ride like hell.'

It suddenly dawned on me what he had in mind, the dynamite, it was in one of the panniers. 'Don't be a fool, Posy, there's a way out of this, there always is.'

'Worried about the gold or my soul?'

'Damn the gold, man, it isn't worth your life, it

isn't worth anyone's life; we should have left it be.'

'Too late for that now, but you're right about one thing, it isn't worth a life, never was. Now get.'

'Posy. . . .'

'Wes, I sold my soul to the Devil for what's in those bags, and now I'm going to cut a deal and buy it back. So run or come to Hell with me if you've a mind to.'

There was a look in his eyes that went beyond the physical pain of the bullet wounds. Posy Tobin was hurting bad from a far deeper wound than ever I could have inflicted upon him. He moved the muzzle of the gun away from me and on to the nearest leather bag.

'Run or stay and stick your fingers in your ears, partner; in a moment there's going to be one hell of a bang. It's your choice.'

I slowly backed off. 'So long, Posy, I wish it could have been some other way.'

'You and me both. So long. . . .'

Then I was running my limping run, the heavy bag banging against my thigh as I tried to cover the ground faster than my legs would take me. I reached the canyon rim and did not look back, grabbing Maria by the arm and hurrying her on down towards the distant trees where the horses were tied. We didn't quite make it.

I distinctly heard the pistol shot but not so clearly the explosion that followed it. That was

Ride a Long Shadow

muffled at first, growing to a roar that sent small chunks of the Chisos skyward to rain down and all around us. The ground shook and the roar had not stilled when a great rush of wind seemed to leap up and out over the canyon rim and race after the woman and me, catching us midstride and sending us flying, falling into the sagebrush and the creosote bushes that covered the rocky floor of the lower ground. I covered Maria with my body, held her shaking shoulders and waited for the calm that I knew for certain would follow the madness of Posy's last bullet.

The quiet eventually came, washed over us in the form of a clean, fresh breeze, cleansed of dust and nitro residue. With an effort, I stood up and helped the still trembling Maria to her feet. She stared at me and I shrugged my shoulders not knowing quite what to say to her. I took her hand in mine and together we walked back to the canyon's rim and looked down. It was as if it had never been. Where once had been a deep gorge, there was now a giant landfill of rock and granite where the canyon's walls had caved in on themselves, covering Posy and Jim Bowie's gold in thousands of tons of boulders and loose rubble.

'Your friend was down there?' she asked, a slight huskiness in her soft voice, the accent more pronounced than usual.

Ride a Long Shadow

I thought about that for a long minute before answering.

'Yes, my friend was down there and I guess that's where he will stay.'

I turned away from the rim and walked back down the ridge. Soon the rains would come again and, as the seasons passed, yellow wild flowers would grow in the crevices, scrub and piñon would root over Posy's grave, deer would graze it. And eagles hunt over it. A man could have a lot less. That growth would be his only marker, that and the memory of him I would carry with me all of my days.

We caught up the bay and the chestnut, but could not find the pack horse, only a broken halter still tied to the low, grey mesquite tree. He was running free somewhere and would, like the mules we also released, make some sort of a home for himself in the Chisos. We kept the burro though, tying off the pannier and our gear on his sturdy back. There were fifteen bars of gold, two of silver and two rotting leather sacks filled with Spanish gold coin in that bag, enough money to last a man forever.

Before we broke camp the next morning, I held Maria close to me and whispered words she wanted to hear, then I saddled the horses and we rode down and out of the Chisos Mountains and into Mexico heading south-east for the Sabinas

Ride a Long Shadow

River, San Miguel and the place she called her home.

Epilogue

I had wanted to split the gold evenly with Maria, but she would have none of it at all unless she could have only what she needed for herself and for the mission. I don't believe that she really wanted any of it, thinking it was tainted in some way as maybe it was. In the end she accepted three gold bars and one silver. I delivered her into the safe-keeping of the very relieved Franciscan priest who met us at the door of the Mission Hospital. Church bells rang in the village and the *alcalde* fêted me and blessed me for returning his daughter safely to him. I hadn't known, she had never spoken of her home other than to say she wanted me to take her there. We made love one final time in the *hacienda* of her family, serenaded by guitars and songs sung to a background chorus of fireworks and festivities which, I guessed, would go on long after I had left. And leave I did, clutching the silver crucifix she presented me with, riding away with the promise that I would visit with her and that should she ever need me, I would be there at her side. I meant it.

It took me nearly three weeks to get back to the Neuces, my trail diverted twice by the Apache and once by two Mexican bandits who wanted whatever was in the leather pannier. I killed one of them and gave twenty gold pieces to the other, telling him to go home and feed his family, winter was coming. I could imagine Posy Tobin enjoying that course of action.

Jonah and Moke were thrilled at my return as was Theresa, although I could sense a certain distance between us. Whether or not that was because I had gone in the first place, or because, with the telling of my story, she guessed there was more to my relationship with Maria than I had spoken of, I could not tell. In my absence, the rains had finally visited our valley and all of the wells had come in, the windmills filling the tanks to overflowing. The cattle were thriving and we had enough money in the Uvaldi bank to ensure both our and Jonah's future whatever the weather. Things were good along the Neuces.

Two days after my return, we rode out to White Hat Creek, just the two of us, wanting to be alone, away from the boy's constant questioning and old Moke's sorrowful gaze. The water was high and the lower branches of the willows drooped into the

Ride a Long Shadow

current. We dismounted and tied off the horses. I tossed stones into the creek remembering the cracked, dry surface of my last visit. I looked up and away in the direction from which Posy had ridden in out of the heat-haze, and fancifully wondered if he had managed to buy back his soul, guessing that he very likely had done just that. The Devil was a sucker for gold.

'What are you thinking about, Wesley?'

Theresa walked over to me and touched my hand.

'About the things I've done, the men I've killed, the men who have died, about grand gestures, moves I should probably not have made.'

'Yesterday, Wes, they all happened yesterday. This is today, the sun is warm, the sky is blue, the creek is full and there is no one around other than the two of us, not counting a steer or three.' She smiled and gently moved my hand to her soft breast, pulling me closer, I went and the distance between us simply faded away.